Wave
Good-bve

Luna Bay
a ♥ ROXY GiRL series

Wave Good-bye

by Francess Lantz

SCHOLASTIC INC.
New York Toronto London Auckland Sydney
Mexico City New Delhi Hong Kong Buenos Aires

ISBN 0-439-61188-1

12 11 10 9 8 7 6 5 4 3 2 1   3 4 5 6 7 8/0

Printed in the U.S.A.   40

First Scholastic printing, October 2003

Designed by Jackie McKee

For Cliff

acknowledgments

With thanks to Matt Jacobson of Quiksilver Entertainment, Chloe Webb, Stan Witnov, Kendra Marcus, and Alice Alfonsi.

1

*R*ae lifts her surfboard into the back of her mother's pickup truck and straps it down. Mom starts the engine, and Rae jumps into the passenger seat. Together they drive down the winding dirt driveway. Behind them the horse trailer bumps and bounces in the ruts.

When they reach the road, Mom hits the brakes. "Did you tie down your board?" she asks.

"Mom, you ask me that every morning. The answer is always the same—yes."

"Those surfboards are dangerous. One flew off a car on the freeway and smashed right into someone's windshield. The driver easily could have been hurt badly."

"I know, Mom."

How many times has Rae heard that story? It's one of her mother's favorites, along with the one about the surfers who were caught spray-painting graffiti on the lifeguard tower at Carson Beach, and the one about the surfers who got into a brawl outside the Surf-N-Taco.

Mom gets out to check the mailbox. Beside it is a wooden sign with the words BRANDY CANYON STABLES: BOARDING, LESSONS, TRAIL RIDES. That's Mom's business, her pride and joy. She wipes a smudge of dirt off the sign and hops back into the truck.

They pull out onto Brandy Canyon Road and drive through rolling brown hills. White fences line the road, and horses graze under twisted oak trees.

"Bor-ing," Rae says under her breath. Her eyes dart sideways. Did Mom hear?

But her mother is staring straight ahead. Unaware that Rae is watching her, she sighs and pushes a strand of straight brown hair behind her ear. The corners of her mouth are turned down, and there's an empty, far-away look in her eyes.

Rae wonders if her mother is thinking about what happened last night. Rae certainly can't forget it. She was lying in bed, glancing through the latest issue of *Surfer Magazine,* when she heard the sharp crash of shattering glass.

Dropping the magazine, she ran to her bedroom door just in time to hear, "Get a grip on yourself, Sara! There's no reason to get hysterical!"

Her father's voice. Rae froze and held her breath.

"Me?" her mother cried. "You're the one who sounds crazy. What do you expect me to do in Chicago, Jake? The ranch is my whole life."

"That's the problem," Dad shot back. "It was fine when the horses were a hobby. But now they're all you think about. You barely have time to say two words to me."

"Look who's talking! I can count on one hand the times you ate dinner at home last month."

"Watch out, Sara." Dad's voice was as sharp as the blade of a knife. "The way things are going, I might stop coming home all together."

Thinking about it now—and about the red wine stain she had noticed on the dining room wall at breakfast this morning—Rae's stomach tightens into a fist. Sure, her parents argue a lot. But this is the first time her mother has thrown a wineglass. And it's definitely the first time Rae's heard her father say anything about Chicago.

What did he mean when he said, "The way things are going, I might stop coming home all together?" Is he really thinking of leaving? The thought makes Rae feel weak and wobbly inside.

And then she thinks about her sister, Sherri. Did she hear Mom and Dad argue? Probably not. Sherri is twelve, doesn't have a care in the world, and sleeps like a corpse. Still . . . Rae decides to feel her out on the subject later, after Sherri gets home from horseback riding camp.

"Rae. *Rae?* Have you heard a word I've said?"

Rae looks up, blinks her eyes. Her mother is staring at her. "What?"

"I said, I want you to leave surf camp a little early today. I'm taking two mothers and their daughters on a beach ride at three o'clock and I could use your help."

"Mom, I can't just up and leave camp anytime I feel like it. I'm a counselor."

"Assistant counselor," Mom points out. "And you're not even getting paid."

"I am, too," Rae counters. "Lunches every day, and a new wet suit at the end of the summer. Besides, I'm getting a lot of great experience."

Mom snorts a laugh. "At what? Being a beach bum?"

"Mom, get a grip! It's like you're living in some ancient Gidget movie or something. This is the twenty-first century. Surfers are not bums. In fact, some pro surfers make more money than you and Dad combined."

"That's the exception, not the rule," Mom says. "Besides, I'm not just talking about money. When's the last time you saw a surfer reading a book?"

"Not lately," Rae says sarcastically. "It's kind of hard to read when the pages are soaking wet."

"Don't be smart with me, young lady. Surfing isn't going to get you into a good college. It takes top grades to do that."

"Who says I want to go to college?" Rae retorts. "I came in second in the ASA Western Championship. *Second!* Do you know what that means? I could turn pro right now. I could—"

"You are not turning pro!" Mom shouts, banging the steering wheel. The horn honks, startling her as she nearly swerves into a ditch. She slams the brakes and pulls the car onto the road's shoulder.

"Mom!" Rae scolds, turning toward her. "What do you think you're . . . ?"

Her voice trails off. Her mother's got her head down on the steering wheel, and her shoulders are heaving. A sob escapes from her throat.

"Mom? Mom, what's wrong?"

Her mother sits up and shakes her head. "I'm tired, that's all." She reaches in her purse for a tissue and dabs her eyes. "I didn't sleep much last night."

Neither did I, Rae wants to say. But Mom is pulling back onto the road again. "How about a little music?" she says cheerfully, flipping on the radio as if the last thirty seconds hadn't even happened.

Rae doesn't know what to say. So she concentrates on the road that is winding over one last dry, brown hill. And suddenly, in a blaze of blue, there it is, spreading out below her—the ocean. Rae lets out a breath she didn't know she was holding. The sight of the sea stretching to the horizon always makes her feel free, as if anything is possible.

A few minutes later, Mom pulls into the parking lot at Crescent Cove Beach Park. Before the truck has rolled to a complete stop, Rae is throwing open the door. Quickly, she unstraps her board and jogs toward the water.

"Three o'clock," her mother calls. "Be here."

Rae doesn't answer, doesn't even bother to wax her surfboard. She just splashes into the shorebreak, hops on her board, and paddles as fast as she can into the lineup.

"Hey, girlfriend!" a voice calls.

Rae looks up. Her best friend, Luna, is sitting on her board just to the right of Black Rock. Glassy four-foot waves peel left and right from the rock to the shore.

"Hi. Pretty crowded for this time of day," Rae says, motioning to the eight or ten other surfers in the water.

"You should have been here earlier," Luna says. "I had the waves all to myself."

Rae looks away. She doesn't want to, but sometimes she feels so jealous of Luna she could scream. Luna's mother is a former pro surfer, and her parents own Shoreline Surf Shop and run the surf camp. They live over the shop, and Luna's room has a picture-perfect view of the beach. No wonder she's the first one in the water every morning!

But it's more than that. Luna's parents don't think surfers are losers. In fact, they *want* her to become a pro. But Luna isn't sure she wants to. Rae can hardly believe it.

If I had Tuck and Cate for parents, Rae tells herself, *I'd quit high school and spend every waking moment training for the world tour.*

Rae glances over at Luna, who is paying more attention to a passing pelican than to the waves. Suddenly Luna's face brightens. "Here comes David," she announces, pointing to the shore.

David is Luna's boyfriend. They met at the start of the summer—David was in the first session of surf camp—and after working their way through a few bumps and detours, they've been hot and heavy ever since. Rae sighs. It's just one more thing Luna has that she doesn't.

Luna kneels on her board and blows a kiss. David waves and begins paddling out.

It's all too much for Rae. If she has to watch Luna and David make kissy faces at each other, she thinks she'll puke. Instead, she takes off on a curling four-foot wave, whips through four snapping cutbacks, and nails an off-the-lip that sends her flying into the air.

She lands it—and manages a small smile of satisfaction.

But it's not enough. The way she feels today, she wants to surf a ten-foot Pipeline barrel. Or a triple overhead Mavericks bone-crusher. Something that will make her forget everything that's going on at home.

"Hey, Rae, that was *sweet!*" calls her friend Isobel.

Rae grins. If any one of her girlfriends is going to surf Mavericks someday, it will be Isobel. Despite the fact that she was a Colorado snowboarder until a year ago, she totally rocks in big surf.

Rae catches a few more waves and surfs hard. She's completely in the moment, thinking about nothing except how the wave is breaking and what her next move will be. For a few blissful minutes, all else is forgotten.

"Earth to Rae! Earth to Rae!"

It's her friend Cricket, and she's sitting on her board, waving her arms like a windmill. "I've been shouting at you for the last five minutes," she says in her usual eighty-mile-an-hour, in-your-face way. "Camp is starting. We have to go in."

Rae nods and starts paddling. Normally she loves working at surf camp. Spending the day at the beach, hanging with her friends, soaking up the surf knowledge of Tuck and Cate—what could be better? But today she's not feeling very chatty or social. And she's definitely not in the mood to be cheering on a bunch of eager-but-lame beginners.

And that's exactly what they are. The last session of surf camp was for intermediate surfers, but this is beginners only. Most of the kids look about ten or twelve years old and completely surf-ignorant. The only exception is David, who got special permission from Luna's parents to stay for another session. He doesn't exactly rip, but thanks to Luna's private tutoring, he's not a beginner anymore, either.

Luna's parents are gathering the group together when a car drives into the parking lot and Kanani jumps out, her long dark hair fluttering in the breeze. "Sorry I'm late," she pants, running over. "My mom got a flat and insisted on changing it herself."

She joins the rest of the girls—Rae, Luna, Isobel, and Cricket. Rae smiles, surveying her crew. They're not only a surf posse, they're best friends. Today they're all wearing T-shirts with the logo Luna designed for them—a curling wave inside a five-sided starburst.

If I can talk to anyone about what's going on at home, it's these girls, Rae tells herself.

But not now. Luna's parents are welcoming the kids to camp and introducing the assistant counselors. The campers—all twenty-five of them—are squirming and giggling. One boy shoves his neighbor. The other boy shoves back.

Rae rolls her eyes. These kids aren't serious about surfing, she can see that. They might as well be at YMCA camp or just hanging out at home.

Home. Rae can't stop thinking about it. Did her father sleep there last night? She didn't see him this morning, but then maybe he was sleeping in. He didn't take Sherri to camp, Rae knows that. She was picked up by her friend Aileen.

"All right, campers," Luna's father says. "Let's break into groups and do some warm-ups."

Rae takes five kids—three girls and two boys—and leads them through some stretches.

"This is boring!" whines a boy with tangled brown hair.

"Okay, how about some jumping jacks?" Rae suggests. "We'll start with twenty. Let's go!"

"When are we going surfing?" asks a skinny girl with braids and braces.

"Yeah, we wanna surf," agrees the brown-haired boy.

"Soon," Rae replies. "But first—"

"Are you the girl who has the beach named after her?" a boy in a Speedo interrupts.

Rae knows he's talking about Luna. She learned to surf right here, at the middle break of Crescent Cove Beach Park. She spent so much time here, in fact, that her father started calling it Luna Bay, and pretty soon the name caught on. Now all the locals call it by that name.

Just another example of Luna's perfect surfing life, Rae thinks. She knows she's feeling sorry for herself, but she can't help it. Luna can spend the whole day in the surf if she wants. But Rae is supposed to help her mother take some stupid tourists on a stupid horseback ride. It's not fair.

"No, I'm not Luna," she says shortly. "I'm Rae. Luna came in sixth in the ASA Western Championship. I came in second."

"Who came in first?" a tall blonde girl asks.

Rae doesn't want to think about Vanessa Haddix, the girl who snagged first place. "Who wants to go surfing?" she asks, hoping to distract the wide-eyed campers.

It works. "We do!" they shout, leaping to their feet like five little jack-in-the-boxes.

Luna's mother is lining up soft-top surfboards at the water's edge. She calls the kids over and gives them a quick lesson in paddling and standing up. Then the campers drag their boards into the shallow water. It's total chaos—twenty-five kids who have almost no idea what they're doing, paddling into each other, falling off, splashing each other, and shrieking.

"Get in there," Luna's dad tells the girls. "Pick two or three kids, push them into some waves, and see if you can get them up. And don't forget to give them lots of encouragement. They're going to need it!"

"This is where we earn our pay," Luna says with a laugh.

"What pay?" Rae asks grumpily. She knows she sounds like her mother, but she can't help it. She gazes over the little kids' heads, out to the lineup. Surfers are taking off on perfect rights and lefts, having the time of their lives. She should be out there with them, she thinks. Instead, she's stuck in the shorebreak with a bunch of goofy grommets.

"It's hard to believe we looked like them once," Cricket says as the girls wade into the water.

"That's because we didn't," Rae replies. "Even when we were beginners, we took surfing seriously."

"Oh, come on, give them a break," Kanani says. "Not everyone wants to be Lisa Anderson. Believe it or not, some people just surf for fun."

Rae knows Kanani is right. She turns to the closest kid, the skinny girl with the braids and braces. "Okay, here comes a wave," she says. "Start paddling!" Rae gives the girl's board a little shove. But the kid barely gets going before she yelps, loses her balance, and falls off.

Rae shakes her head. She knows she should help the next kid she sees—a plump boy in baggy blue trunks—but a sweet little wave is coming her way. Giving in to impulse, she turns to the boy and says, "Give me your board. I'll show you how it's done."

The boy looks surprised, but he does as he's told. Rae jumps on, paddles twice, and stands up. The soft-topped longboard handles like a boat, but she manages a couple of cutbacks, maneuvering around the wide-eyed campers, before the wave closes out.

Rae jumps off and grabs the board. She's met by Luna, who looks perplexed. "What was that about?"

"What?"

"We're supposed to be helping the campers, not showing off," Luna says.

"If I wanted to show off, I'd do a lot more than a couple of lame cutbacks," Rae says with a laugh.

But Luna doesn't join in. "Come on, Rae. I know this isn't your idea of a hot surf session, but—"

Luna's tone reminds Rae of her mother. "Don't lecture me," she grumbles. "Not today, okay?"

Luna frowns at her friend. "What's wrong, Rae?"

Rae wants to tell her, but David is just a couple of feet away, and Luna's dad is looking over as if to say, "Stop goofing off, you two," and the boy whose board Rae borrowed is swimming toward them.

"Nothing," she mutters.

"Rae, come on. I know that look. What's—?"

"Hey, I'm sorry I can't smile all day long like you do," Rae says irritably. "But maybe that's because I don't lead your charmed life."

Luna looks stunned, as if she's been just been slapped. Rae knows she's being a brat, but deep down it feels kind of good to lash out. Before her friend can say anything, Rae jumps on the surfboard and paddles away.

When surf camp ends, Rae grabs her board and heads up the beach. She can't wait to get out of there, away from all those tiresome, noisy, squirmy kids. But it's not just the campers she wants to escape. Since their exchange in the shallow surf, she and Luna haven't said one word to each other. Rae knows she should apologize—she was way out of line, she can't deny it—but she doesn't want to.

Not that Luna wouldn't be sympathetic. Rae knows she would be. But maybe, she decides, that's part of the problem. Rae doesn't want sympathy, especially from Luna "Life Is Good" Martin. She just wants her parents to stop fighting. Even more than that, she wants to surf without anyone telling her she's showing off, or goofing off, or messing up her chances to get into a good college.

That's why, when her mother calls to her from across the parking lot, Rae ignores her and keeps walking.

"Rae," Mom calls, "where are you going? I expected you here fifteen minutes ago. I need you to help me saddle the horses!"

Rae knows she's letting her mother down. She knows Mom is seething. And she knows she's going to pay for this later. But she doesn't care. Surfboard tucked under her arm like a security blanket, she breaks into a run. She's going surfing, and nobody's going to stop her.

2

*R*ae scrambles over the rocks that separate Luna Bay from North Beach. She can't hear her mother's voice now, can't see her mother, and knows Mom can't see her.

"I'm free," she says out loud.

Now it's just a matter of finding some good surf. North Beach isn't breaking, so she continues on. There's a long stretch of boring beach break, but Rae isn't looking for boring today. She wants to go wild, really break out and do something extreme—something that will erase last night and this morning from her mind.

Then she sees it—the pier. There's a nice left that breaks away from the pier on the south side. That's where she and her friends usually surf. There's also a right that breaks on the north side, directly into the pilings. If you've got the talent and the guts, you can "shoot the pier"—ride the wave between the pilings and come out the other side.

Rae's never tried it, but it looks like a rush. That is, *if* you make it. If you mess up, you could end up wrapped around a piling—or worse.

"I can do this," Rae says with a confidence she's trying hard to feel.

She paddles out and joins the small, select group of surfers—all male—who favor the break. They glance at her skeptically, but don't say anything. Rae takes it as a challenge. *I'll show them,* she tells herself. *When this afternoon is over, I'll have their respect.*

She floats on her board, watching which waves the guys take, how they break, how the best of them maneuver between the pilings and shoot out the other side. Finally, she decides she's ready. Ignoring the fluttering in her stomach and the slamming in her chest, she waits for a well-formed, uncrowded wave and takes off.

She drops in, bottom-turns, gets her bearings. Piece of cake!

The pier is getting closer. She crouches down, pulls into the pocket of the wave—the spot that will give her the most speed and power.

The pilings are looming, looking bigger and more solid than she ever imagined. Her heart is thumping like a cornered rabbit's, and she can't help thinking about the razor-sharp mussels that line the pilings. They could slash right through a wet suit—or a face. But a few scars would be nothing compared to what would happen if you collided with the pier. The possibilities flash through Rae's mind—bruises, broken bones, brain damage, death.

Now! Rae rockets between two pilings, out of the sunlight and into shadow. She cuts back, avoiding the second pair of pilings, then—yikes! The wave closes out, forcing her to turn toward the shore—and a huge, slimy, seaweed- and mussel-covered piling!

It's either bail or crash, so she flings herself sideways off her board. She hits the water, bounces off a piling, and starts swimming like a lunatic toward the sunlight. Her leash catches on a cluster of mussels, but she yanks it free and emerges from beneath the pier just as another wave is about to crash on her. She dives under it, comes up, and sees a momentary lull in the surf. Quickly, she retrieves her board, leaps on, and speed-paddles to safety.

She's sitting outside the lineup on the south side of the pier, trying desperately to catch her breath, when she sees a familiar face. Luna is paddling toward her!

"Are you out of your mind!" her friend cries. "You could have been killed!"

"Yeah, but I wasn't," Rae says, panting. She pats her arms and legs to prove it to herself. Tomorrow she'll probably have some major bruises, but for now, riding on a burst of adrenaline, she's feeling no pain. "How'd it look?" she asks.

"Insane," Luna answers. "Awesome!"

Rae grins. "Not bad for a first try."

Luna laughs and shakes her head. Then her expression turns serious. "You've been acting crazy all morning. Come on, Rae, spill. What's going on?"

Rae takes a deep breath. "It's Mom and Dad. They had a huge blowout last night—even worse than usual. Mom threw a glass against the wall, and Dad threatened to move out."

"Oh, Rae!" Luna says with a sigh. "No!"

"I don't know if he was serious. Mom said something about Chicago."

"Chicago!"

Rae nods. "And then this morning, on the way to the beach, Mom and I got into a big fight and she burst into tears. Luna, my mother never cries—not even the time she got thrown from a horse and broke her wrist."

"Maybe you should talk to her," Luna suggests.

"Not today. She wanted me to help her take some tourists on a beach ride and I bailed. She's ready to kill me."

Luna thinks it over. "Let's go to my house. Then later, after your mom has had a few hours to cool down, I'll get my mom to call her and ask if you can sleep over."

For the first time all day, Rae manages a heartfelt smile. Why, she asks herself, was she so snippy with her best friend this morning?

"Thanks," she says. "I'm sorry I was such a pain in the butt back at camp. I was pretty stressed, I guess."

Luna smiles. "No worries." She offers her fist and Rae taps it with her own. "Let's stop for smoothies on the way home," Luna says. "My treat."

Smooth Moves is packed with surfers, tourists, and mothers with screaming toddlers. Rae and Luna lean their boards against the wall outside and join the line that stretches almost out the door.

"I'm having a Peanut Butter Fudge Fury," Rae says. "After my close encounter with the pier, I deserve it."

"Don't tell me you girls tried to shoot the pier," says a voice behind them.

Rae and Luna turn around. It's Shane Fox, a local surfer who dropped out of high school last year to join the pro tour.

"I not only tried, I made it," Rae replies. "Well . . . almost."

Shane looks concerned. "That place is dangerous. I wouldn't want you girls to get hurt. Of course, after Pipe, coming back to the pier is sort of a letdown for me."

Rae and Luna exchange a glance. Shane has always been way too impressed with himself. In the past, Rae has written him off as an arrogant egotist. But after his better-than-average first year on the pro tour—including an impressive third-place showing at Pipe—she has to admit he's got good reason to be cocky. He's one hot surfer, and not bad-looking, either—blue eyes, spiky brown hair with blond tips, and a lean, wiry body.

"I hear you came in second in the Championship, Rae," he continues. "I didn't know you had it in you."

"Thanks—I think," Rae replies. "I guess you've had a pretty good year yourself."

"Just wait until next year," he says. "I'm going to blow those old-timers out of the water. It's time for some new blood in the top five."

"Poor Shane. So shy and unassuming," Luna quips. "You should work on building up your self-confidence."

Shane chuckles. "I guess that sixth-place showing really helped pump up *your* self-esteem," he says.

Everyone expected Luna to do much better than sixth in the Championship. But instead of showing off her impressive power moves, she chose to soul-surf the contest, even giving up the wave of the day so Rae could take it.

Rae frowns. Luna has tried to explain her decision—

something about surfing with your heart—but Rae still doesn't quite get it. If you have a chance to win, she figures, why not go for it?

"I was happy with my performance," Luna says.

But Shane doesn't seem to be listening. He's looking at Rae, checking her out as if she's a surfboard he's thinking of buying. "You're growing up," he says thoughtfully.

Rae can feel her cheeks growing warm. "I'm sixteen," she says. "How about you?"

"Eighteen. Is that strawberry-blonde hair of yours real?"

"Sure. How about those blond tips? All natural, right?"

He snickers. "What are you doing this evening?"

Rae can't believe her ears. Is Shane asking what she thinks he's asking? "Not much. Why?"

"Just wondering if you want to go surfing with me. You might be able to pick up a few tips, some things that will help you the next time you compete against Vanessa Haddix."

"Rae . . ." Luna says, and Rae knows it means, "You've got to be kidding!"

But Rae figures, why not? Sure, Shane is full of himself. That doesn't mean he doesn't have his good points, like hot surf moves and a hot look to match. Besides, if he wants to share what he's learned on the pro tour, she'd be a fool to say no. What's that phrase her mother always uses? Don't look a gift horse in the mouth.

"Sounds good to me," she says.

He smiles, revealing a set of gleaming white teeth. "I'll see you around seven at Triples," he says, using the local name for the three beaches of Crescent Cove Beach Park. "Look for me in the water."

They've reached the front of the line, so Rae and Luna order and step back to wait for their smoothies. "What are you thinking?" Luna whispers in Rae's ear. "That guy is so in love with himself it makes me sick."

"But think what he can teach me—about surfing, about the tour, about all kinds of stuff. Anyway, what can it hurt to go surfing with him just this once?"

"I thought you were sleeping over."

"I am," Rae says. "After dinner we'll tell your parents we're going for a walk. Then I'll meet Shane for an hour or so. No big deal, right?"

Luna purses her lips, hesitates, then shrugs. "No big deal."

Rae grins. Maybe she's nuts, but she can't help feeling a little flattered that Shane picked her over Luna. Luna's the one with the perfect surfer looks—streaky blonde hair, gray-green eyes, and a tall, willowy body. Rae, on the other hand, with her short strawberry-blonde hair, pixie face, and slim hips, rarely attracts many male glances. Not that she ever cared. Surfing with her girlfriends has always been more important to her than boys. But still . . .

Rae perks up when she hears Shane ordering his smoothie. "I'll have what she's having," he says, glancing back at her and smiling.

A funny tingle shoots down Rae's spine. She can hardly wait for tonight.

3

You remember the time Shane got suspended for skipping an entire week of school?" Luna asks as she and Rae stroll down Surf Street that evening.

Rae giggles. "The rumor was he and his big brother went on a surf trip to Baja."

"They say he forged his mother's name on the note. Only he spelled it wrong!"

"Do you think that's true?" Rae asks. "I mean, Shane doesn't seem like the type to do something that dumb."

"Maybe it had nothing to do with smarts," Luna suggests. "Maybe he just didn't care."

Rae thinks that over. She's never said more than five words to Shane until this afternoon, but she does know one thing about him: He lives to surf. And that, Rae has noticed, often puts teenagers at odds with the adult world. Eventually, maybe you just stop caring. Then you do whatever you please, and if the grownups don't like it, too bad.

Rae thinks about her parents. She wishes she could stop caring so much about them. But the truth is, she's dying to know what's going on at home. Did her dad spend the night somewhere else? Are Mom and Dad still fighting? And what's all this about Chicago?

Rae considers calling home on the off chance that Sherri might answer. Then she could get an update on the Mom and Dad wars. But what if Mom picks up? It was a miracle Luna's mom convinced her to let Rae sleep over. Rae doesn't want to give her a chance to change her mind.

"I'm going for a jog," Luna says. "I'll see you back at my house in an hour or so, okay?"

"Sure you don't want to come with me?" Rae asks.

Luna shakes her head. "Shane asked you. Besides," she adds, gesturing toward the surfboard Rae is carrying under her arm, "in case you forgot, you're using my board."

Rae smiles. She knows that's just an excuse. Luna has other surfboards. She just doesn't want to hang out with Shane. And that's fine with Rae. She knows Luna doesn't like him much. Not that she didn't feel the same way at one point. But after their exchange at Smooth Moves this afternoon, well, Rae wants to give him a chance.

"Later," she calls as Luna jogs away. Then she walks to the water's edge and scans the surf for Shane. He didn't say exactly where he'd be, but the waves look pretty good peeling off Black Rock—three to four feet and hollow.

Then she spots him. He's wearing his trademark custom-made wet suit with the yellow collar and sleeves. It really makes him stand out in the surf. She sees him take off and disappear into a small, pitching barrel. He flies out the other side and proceeds to carve the wave as if it were a platter of Thanksgiving turkey.

Whoa, Rae thinks. *He was hot before, but the year on the tour has set him on fire!*

Heart pumping, Rae paddles out. She wants to impress Shane with her surfing ability, to make him think *whoa,* just like she did. But after the ride she just witnessed, she feels like a beginner.

"Hi," she calls, joining Shane in the lineup.

"Hey," he replies. "Did you see my last ride?"

"Yes! You looked awesome!"

Shut up, she tells herself. *You sound like a groupie.*

There's a set rolling in. Time to show Shane what she's got. She takes off on the first wave and pulls into the tube, but it's too small to get covered. Instead, the lip smacks her head like a curtain closing on a Broadway bomb. She hangs on, recovers, and does a floater across the soup before pulling out.

Lame, she thinks. *I can surf better than that.*

Shane thinks so, too. "You can do better than that," he says. "All you need is a few lessons from the master."

"Tommy Curren?" she quips.

"Yeah, right. Like he's not totally washed up already." He pauses. "Well, what do you say? Do you want me to coach you or don't you?"

"You want to give me some pointers?"

"For starters. Then, if I think you have potential, we'll get serious."

Rae has never had a coach, never even thought about it. She feels flattered that Shane thinks she's worth spending time on. But what will it entail, exactly? She wants to ask, but doesn't know how.

She decides to go for a generic response. "I'm always interested in improving my surfing."

"Then listen up. The pro tour is way more competitive than anything you've ever experienced. Let's be honest—you're not ready."

Rae knows she must look crestfallen, because Shane adds quickly, "I'm not saying that to hurt you. I just don't want you going out there and getting your butt kicked. Those pro chicks are vicious. You've got a long way to go before you can compete with them."

"But—"

"Look, Rae, you've got lots of natural talent. It just needs refining. When you're ready, I'll be the first to tell you."

Rae leans forward eagerly. She feels like she'd do practically anything to hear him say, "You're ready." And yet a part of her holds back. Shane may be a top surfer, but that doesn't mean he knows how to coach. And why would he want to? What's in it for him?

"After the Championship, a couple of surf company reps gave me their business cards," she says. "RippedWear and Blade Surfboards. I think they both have surf teams. Maybe they're going to want me to join."

Shane gazes at her disdainfully. "RippedWear is about to go bankrupt. And Blade already sponsors more surfers than they can handle. You won't get much promotion if you sign with them."

"Oh," Rae replies. Shane not only knows how to surf, she realizes, he knows the business side of the surfing world, too.

"I'm sponsored by Edge Surfwear," he tells her. "They're talking about putting out a wetsuit based on my design. It'll say SHANE FOX in yellow letters right across the front."

"Cool!"

He smiles. "Let's catch some waves and I'll give you some pointers."

Rae spends the next hour surfing her heart out, then paddling back to the lineup to hear Shane tell her that her bottom turns are weak, her cutbacks are sketchy, and the big air she thinks she's catching can only be measured in millimeters.

Rae checks her watch. She was supposed to meet Luna at the house ten minutes ago. "I've got to go," she says.

"Why? There's at least another hour of daylight."

"I'm sleeping over at Luna's house. She's expecting me."

Shane looks disappointed. "I thought we'd stop by Java Jones for a mocha."

Java Jones, the trendiest coffeehouse in Crescent Cove? That's like a date, almost. "Well, maybe a quick one," she says.

Shane flashes his toothy smile—half little boy, half shark. They paddle in, dry off, and carry their boards down Shoreline Drive to the coffeehouse. It's furnished with overstuffed olive-green sofas and chairs. The purple walls are covered with an assortment of funky junk—an old bicycle, a French horn, dog-eared sheet music, a moth-eaten overcoat. In the corner, a twentysomething guy with dreadlocks is playing blues guitar.

Rae and Shane order mochas and find an empty corner. Rae sinks into an easy chair and sips her drink. Shane stretches his legs across the coffee table. "How are things at Crescent Cove High?" he asks with a smirk.

"Same old same old," she says. Like either of them cares about boring old CCH! "Tell me about the tour," she urges.

He gazes up at the ceiling, remembering. "You haven't lived 'til you've surfed Pipe. Or Tavarua—now that's a killer wave."

Hawaii, Fiji—it all sounds so exotic! Rae would cut off her right arm to travel to those places, let alone compete there.

"And the people?"

He shrugs. "You meet all types. Nice guys, loners, jokers, kooks. Doesn't matter. As far as I'm concerned, they all fall into two categories—winners and losers."

Rae doesn't know what to think. Shane sounds awfully cold. Still, she's got to admire his determination. He knows what he wants and he's going to get it. She has no doubt about that.

"I want it, too," she says, half to herself.

"What's that?"

"A first-place trophy."

Shane grins. "That's the attitude. Talent's not enough. You gotta have that killer instinct."

Is that true? Rae wonders. And what exactly does it mean? Maybe Shane can teach her.

She takes a sip of her mocha and notices him looking at her. "I love reddish-blonde hair," he says softly.

Rae knows she's grinning like a moron. "I—I look

like my dad—the hair, that is," she blurts out. "The rest of me is a lot like my grandmother on my mother's side. The only one I don't look anything like is my mom. I mean, we're complete opposites—looks, interests, personality, everything. She doesn't even like the water."

"No?"

He doesn't sound very interested, but Rae can't seem to shut up. "No, she's into horses. We've got ten of them, plus five more that board at our stables. Talk about stink! When the wind is right, it's like a fertilizer factory."

Suddenly he looks interested. "You live on a ranch?"

"Yeah, up off Brandy Canyon Road. Do you ride?"

"No, but I'd like to try it sometime."

Suddenly Brandy Canyon Stables doesn't seem like such a dreary place. "Sure," she says brightly. "Anytime."

Shane doesn't answer. He's turning toward a group of four boys who are edging toward them. They're all about thirteen years old and wearing surf T-shirts. "Hey, Shane," one of them mumbles. "Can we have your autograph?"

"Sure," he says. One of them thrusts a pen in Shane's direction, and he scribbles his name on the napkin.

"Thanks," the bravest of them mutters. "You are like, my idol, man."

"Yeah," another boy says, "you totally rip!"

Shane grins. "See you in the surf, guys."

The boys look like they're going to faint at the very thought. They stumble backward, then turn and practically run out the door.

Rae gazes at Shane, impressed. "You're a hero to those kids."

He laughs. "But not a role model, I hope. That would be way too much work."

Rae laughs, too, then suddenly remembers she was supposed to be at Luna's house almost an hour ago. "Shane, I have to go."

"Sure. Listen, give me your phone number. We'll go surfing again soon."

Rae has to go up to the counter to get a pen. She notices her hand trembling as she writes. It's so unlike her, and she doesn't know what's happening. She doesn't let boys get to her. What's different about Shane?

It's not that she likes him or anything. After all, he *is* awfully stuck-up. Although now that she thinks of it, maybe it's not conceit but confidence. And maybe it's something you've got to have to make it on the pro tour.

In any case, she can't deny he knows a lot about surfing. And what's amazing is that he seems to want to share it with her. Well, why not? She won't say no.

She rushes back to Shane and hands him her number. "See you soon," he says with a little half-smile.

Their eyes lock and she feels her ears start to sweat. "I hope so," she whispers.

4

You went surfing with Shane Fox?" Cricket cries, almost choking on her breakfast of Coke and Oreos.

It's dawn, the morning after the sleepover, and Rae and Luna are driving to Carson Beach with Kanani, Isobel, and Cricket. According to the Internet surf reports that Cricket pours over every morning, the surf should be pumping.

Rae shrugs. "Yeah, we surfed together. Why not?"

"Mr. I'm-A-Golden-Surf-God Fox?" Kanani asks. "Why would you want to hang out with him?"

"Are you serious?" Rae replies. "Shane is on the tour. I can learn a lot from him."

"Like what?" Isobel asks. "How to be a stuck-up snot?"

"That's kind of harsh," Rae shoots back. "Sure,

Shane likes to boast, but you gotta admit, he's got a lot to boast about. I mean, third place in his first Pipe Masters. Come on!"

"He's an up-and-comer," Luna concedes. "No one's denying that, but—"

"Shane can be really nice, too," Rae jumps in. "Not everybody sees that side, but it's there. Like when we were in Java Jones and some little kids asked him for his autograph. He could have blown them off, but he didn't."

Isobel is looking at Rae with a knowing smile. "You've got the hots for him, don't you?"

"No way!" she protests. "I just—"

"You can't fool me. Look at you. You're practically drooling."

"Oh, please," Rae scoffs. But then she remembers the way Shane looked at her—looked inside her, almost—and said, "I love reddish-blonde hair." He was so serious, so intense, so passionate. The memory makes her skin tingle.

"Look at her!" Cricket exclaims. "She's blushing. Now we know it's true."

"Well, he *is* pretty handsome," Luna points out, "in a cocky underwear model kind of way."

"Stop it," Rae grumbles. "You know I've never been the type to get all goofy over a cute boy—or any boy, for that matter."

The girls know it's true. Rae has had plenty of friends who are boys, but no boyfriends. Luna asked her about it once, but Rae couldn't really explain why. Maybe it's because she's so focused on her surfing, or because she refuses to dress up and play the flirting game. Whatever it is, she's never had many dates and she's never really cared.

But will things be different with Shane? Rae pushes the question out of her mind.

"All I'm saying is," she continues, "I'm not easily impressed. But Shane's surfing impresses me, okay?"

"Okay, okay," Kanani says as Luna pulls into the dirt parking lot above Carson Beach. "Enough about Shane Fox. Let's check out the surf."

The girls jump out of the car and survey the beach. To their delight, it's empty—and so are the waves. With whoops of joy, they grab their boards and run down the wooden staircase to the sand.

"Hey, what's that?" Isobel asks, pausing and peering into the mist.

The girls follow her gaze. A small dark shape is moving in the dunes about a hundred yards up the beach.

"A coyote?" Rae suggests.

"Too small," Luna says. "Maybe a dog."

"Or a cat," Cricket adds.

"Or a mountain lion, hungry for tasty young surfer girls," Kanani declares.

The girls laugh. Then, turning their attention to the waves, they slip on their wet suits and splash into the surf.

The waves are three to four feet high, with an occasional five-footer. Kanani takes the first wave. It's small but fast. She walks to the nose and arches her back in classic longboard style.

"Sweet!" Luna says.

Cricket takes off next. She weaves up and down the wave, sending rooster tails of spray in every direction, never stopping until every inch of open face has been shredded.

A five-footer is rolling in. "Charge it!" Luna calls to Isobel.

Isobel drops in and bottom-turns hard. She's taller than the other girls, heavier and stronger. She muscles her way up the face and leans hard into a huge backside cutback.

Rae can't wait any longer. She paddles into position and takes off, trying to imagine how Shane would surf the wave if he were here. She drops into the pocket, picks up speed, then shoots to the lip and catches air.

Kanani and Cricket are paddling out. "Go, girl, go!" Kanani screams as Rae rockets past her.

"Who-hoo!" Cricket whoops, arms in the air.

Later, back in the lineup, Kanani says, "You were on fire, Rae."

"See?" she replies. "I told you I could learn something from Shane Fox."

"What else has he taught you?" Cricket asks with a wry smile.

Rae rolls her eyes. "Here we go again."

"*What?*" Cricket says, all wide-eyed innocence.

Rae laughs and reaches out to shove Cricket off her board. Suddenly a sleek, black head pops up out of the water.

"Ahh!" Rae shrieks, leaping back.

As quickly as it appeared, the head disappears.

"What was that?" Cricket asks anxiously.

"A harbor seal, I think," Rae stammers. "Or—or maybe—"

"Hey!" cries Kanani.

The girls spin around just in time to see a wet black-and-brown dog scramble onto Kanani's surfboard. Panting and wagging its tail, it eyes her expectantly.

"Where did you come from?" Kanani asks in astonishment. She reaches out a hesitant hand. The dog moves closer and licks her fingers.

"Cute!" Isobel exclaims.

"It must be the animal we saw in the dunes," Luna says.

"The mountain lion, huh?" Rae teases.

"No collar," Kanani points out. She scratches the dog behind its ear. "Where's your owner?"

"He's a funny-looking guy," Rae remarks.

The dog has a black body and a reddish-brown face and paws. His body is long and barrel-shaped, while his legs are short and stubby.

"His face looks like a Lab, except for those floppy ears," Isobel says. "And check out his legs! Do you think he's part basset hound?"

"Or corgi, maybe," Rae says. "You know, those dogs the Queen of England owns? I saw a photo of her with a whole pack of them once."

"Look at that face," Kanani says, smiling as she pats his head. "He looks young, hardly more than a puppy."

The dog picks that moment to leap off the surfboard. He lands in the water with a plop and begins paddling his paws, barking excitedly.

"What's with him?" Cricket wonders. "Hey, what is it, boy?"

Rae follows the dog's gaze. Three seagulls are floating nearby. "I think he wants those birds," she says.

"No, no, no," Luna scolds. "No birds. Why don't you see if he likes to surf?" she asks Kanani.

"Me? Why me?"

"Because you have the longboard. Go on, see if he'll ride with you."

"Come here, pup," Kanani calls. "Come on, boy."

The dog looks at the birds, then back at Kanani. Finally, he swims back and leaps onto her board. She waits for a small, gentle wave. Then she gets on her knees and starts paddling. The dog barks, but he doesn't jump off.

And then they're riding—Kanani in back and the little dog in front, barking and hopping up and down. Suddenly he jumps too close to the edge, slips, and slides off into the water. Undaunted, he turns around and paddles back toward the lineup. A barreling wave pitches over him and the girls hold their breath, but he pops out the other side and keeps swimming.

"He's like a harbor seal," Rae laughs.

"Except with paws instead of flippers," Luna says.

"Here, boy!" they all call. "Good dog!"

He paddles back to them and climbs onto Rae's board. He gazes up at her with his big brown eyes, looking so cute she wants to hug him. "Where's your owner?" she asks, scratching his chin.

Kanani paddles back to the lineup. "I wish he was ours," she says wistfully.

"What's your name?" Rae asks. "Surfer? Swimmer?"

"Rover?" Luna suggests. "Lad? Shrimp? Shorty?"

"If he were mine, I'd name him Barrels," Rae says. "You all saw him swim through that barreling wave, and besides, he's built like a barrel."

"I like that!" Cricket exclaims. "Hey, Barrels! Come here, Barrels!"

To everyone's amazement, the dog jumps from

Rae's board to Cricket's board. Cricket draws back, a look of alarm on her face. "I didn't think he'd really come. I like dogs, but—I don't know—they make me nervous."

"Oh, come on, look at him," Luna says. "He wouldn't hurt a sand flea."

Cricket looks. Barrels's tail is thumping rhythmically against her board. "I've never had a pet," she says, extending a hesitant hand. The dog shoves his head under her fingers. She giggles and gives him an experimental scratch.

"Maybe Barrels really *is* his name," Rae says.

"Yeah, maybe you're psychic, Rae." Isobel chuckles.

"Come on," Kanani urges. "Are we going to talk or are we going to surf?"

For the next hour, the girls take turns catching waves and playing with Barrels. Eventually, more surfers paddle out. They all ask about Barrels and call him over, but to the girls' delight, he refuses to go.

"If we can't find his owner, let's keep him," Isobel says.

"How can we do that?" Rae asks. "We all live in different places."

"So we'll take turns keeping him," she replies. "One week at each house. And when we go surfing, we'll bring him along."

"*If* we can't find the owner," Luna reminds them.

The girls nod in agreement. "Right," they all say.

So they head in, Barrels riding on Kanani's board, and search the beach for the owner. But there are only five or six people on the beach, and none of them know Barrels.

"Poor guy," Rae says, leaning down to nuzzle Barrels's head. "You're lost."

"I'll make some posters and put them up," Luna says. "Maybe his owner will see one of them and call us."

"Until then, he's ours," Isobel says, barely able to hide her pleasure.

Rae has to admit she's pleased, too. "Come on, Barrels," she calls. "It's time to go to surf camp."

The girls start up the stairs to the parking lot. Barrels scampers after them, panting and wagging his tail.

"The kids are going to looooove you!" Kanani exclaims.

Rae leans down to give Barrels a pat. "We do, too," she says.

5

Luna turns off Brandy Canyon Road and bumps up the rutted dirt driveway that leads to Rae's house. Beside her, Rae hugs Barrels to her chest.

"How do you like your new home, pup?" Rae coos. "It's not the beach, but it'll have to do."

Barrels pricks up his nose and sniffs. In the distance, a horse whinnies. Barrels's ears pop to attention.

"Don't get too comfy, Barrels," Luna says. "You're coming to my house next week—unless we find your owner first, that is."

"I hope we don't," Rae confides.

"Me, too. But we have to put up some posters, maybe run an ad in the newspaper. Just imagine if Barrels was your dog and you lost him. You'd be so sad."

Rae has to agree. She gives Barrels a final hug as Luna stops the car. The Perrault family dogs—an Australian shepherd and a Boston terrier—come bounding out of a nearby corral, barking and wagging their tails.

"Hey, Harley! Hey, Nipper!" Rae calls, throwing open the car door. "Meet Barrels!"

Barrels jumps out and the dogs do their getting-to-know-you routine—lots of sniffing, wagging, and peeing on fence posts. They're still at it when Rae's little sister, Sherri, walks out of the house, her shoulder-length red hair partially covered by a cowboy hat.

"Oh, what a sweetie!" she cries when she spots Barrels. "Who does he belong to?"

"Us," Rae says. "For the week anyway. We found him at Carson Beach. He swam out to the lineup and the next thing we knew, he was full-on surfing with Kanani."

"No way!" Sherri exclaims. "Where's his owner?"

"That's what we're trying to find out," Luna replies. "I'm going to stop by the art store and buy some poster paper. I'll call you later, Rae."

Luna is turning the car around as Rae's mom strides out of the house. "Where'd that dog come from?" she demands.

"Rae found him on the beach," Sherri says. "Can we keep him?"

"Absolutely not!" She turns to Rae. "What's going on?"

"Just what Sherri said," Rae answers, wondering why her mother is so bent out of shape. "The girls and I are going to take turns keeping him until we find his owner. We drew straws and I get him for the first week."

"Not a chance," Mom snaps. "You're going to have to call your friends and tell them to come get him."

"But why? He won't be any trouble. He can sleep in the stables with Harley and Nipper. See," she adds, pointing to the dogs, who are romping across the front lawn, "they like each other."

Mom is shaking her head like a metronome. "No, no, no. There's too much going on around here already. I can't handle another dog."

"But, Mom—" Sherri whines.

"I said I can't handle it!" she shouts, holding her head as if she's trying to keep it from exploding.

Rae stares at her mother, trying to ignore the sick feeling in the pit of her stomach. Mom has never been the easygoing type, but this is totally over the top. Between yesterday's crying jag and today's freakout, Rae doesn't know what to think. Is Mom having a nervous breakdown or something?

Mom looks back and forth between her daughters' stunned faces. Then, slowly, she drops her hands and says in a worn-out whisper, "I'm sorry. I really am."

"Mom, what is it?" Rae asks. "What's wrong?"

Her mother frowns and looks down at her shoes. Then, finally, she says, "Come inside, girls. We have to talk."

The walk from the driveway to the living room feels

like a hundred miles. Rae tries to pretend she doesn't know what her mother is going to say, but she can't fool herself. It has something to do with her parents' marriage, and it isn't good.

Mom lowers herself heavily onto the beige sofa. Nervously fingering the *Horses of the World* book on the coffee table, she waits for Rae and Sherri to sit on the loveseat opposite her. Then she sighs deeply and says, "Girls, your father and I have decided to separate."

Deep down in the most secret part of her heart, Rae had kept alive a tiny flame of hope. Now, like a boot heel stamping out a cigarette butt, it's instantaneously extinguished.

"But why?" she cries, blurting out her worst fear. "Are you in love with someone else? Or Dad—is he cheating on you?"

Mom laughs humorlessly. "Nothing that dramatic. We just disagree on . . . well, on practically everything. You see, your father never wanted to live in the country. He did that for me. But over the years, I think it's really frustrated him. Now his company wants to transfer him to Chicago, and he wants to go."

"He wants us to move to Chicago?" Sherri asks in disbelief.

"That's what he told me. But I said you girls were happy here. And besides, what would I do in a big city like that?"

The last thing Rae wants is to move to the middle of

the country, miles away from the ocean. But for her father's sake, she says, "You could have horses if we lived in the suburbs."

"Sure, and ride maybe five or six months out of the year. It snows out there, Rae, real blizzards. Anyway, the timing couldn't be worse. The property next door is for sale. If I bought it, I could expand the stables, take in more boarders. Your father says we don't have enough money. But if we took out a loan, I know I could make it work."

Rae doesn't know what to say. She's heard her father complaining that he didn't get a raise this year, that his company was laying people off. Maybe he has to move to Chicago or risk getting fired, she tells herself.

And what about the stables? Is her mother's plan a good one? Will she be able to pull it off without Dad around to provide a steady income?

Questions keep circling around Rae's brain, but they're quickly forgotten when Sherri bursts into tears and cries, "I don't want Daddy to move away! I want everything to stay the way it's always been!"

"Oh, honey," Mom says, reaching over to touch her hand, "I do, too. But sometimes people grow apart from each other and—"

"But why?" Rae demands. "Can't you and Dad sit down and talk it out?"

"We've tried that. Somehow our talks always turn into fights."

"Then you're not trying hard enough," Rae insists. "Luna's parents don't fight. They talk things out and compromise. Why can't you and Dad compromise, too?"

"And what?" Mom asks dryly. "Move to . . . I don't know, Nebraska next?" She shakes her head. "It's not that simple, Rae."

"Well, what about counseling?" Rae presses. "Isobel's parents went to a marriage counselor once. And look at them. They're still together."

"We tried that, too," Mom says, sounding defeated. "Girls, you have to understand. I don't want things to change, either. But they're going to. That's just the way it is. We'll just have to deal with it together."

Sherri is still sobbing, so upset she isn't even bothering to wipe her runny nose. Rae feels like crying, too. But she's afraid that if she starts, she'll never be able to stop. Gulping back the burning lump in her throat, she whispers, "Where's Dad? I want to talk to him."

"Me, too." Sherri sniffles.

Mom stiffens. "I don't know where your father is. He left without telling me. He might be in Chicago already, for all I know."

Rae can't believe it. What if she never sees her father again? The thought is too much to bear, and now a painful whimper escapes her throat. But unlike her sister, she doesn't want to fall apart in front of Mom, doesn't want to hear any more of her explanations or excuses. Instead, she leaps to her feet, runs into her bedroom, and slams the door.

Throwing herself on her bed, Rae can't hold back anymore. She's full-on sobbing now, just letting it out. She hears a knock at her door, but she doesn't want to talk to anyone now, *can't* talk to anyone. "Go away!" she cries, shouting not just to the person on the other side of her bedroom door, but to the whole world. "Just go away!"

Much later, when she can't cry anymore, Rae dries her eyes and blows her nose. Then she opens her guitar case and takes out her guitar. She's been playing for years, but she's only recently begun writing songs. She doesn't know what she's doing, really, and she doubts they're any good. Still, it feels so right to think up words and combine them with music—like pulling off the perfect surfing moves on the perfect wave.

Rae's breath is still coming in shaky hiccups. She strums a few chords, searching for a sound that will mirror how she feels inside. When she finds a sequence of chords she likes, she plays it over and over. A phrase pops into her head: caught in the middle.

That's how she feels right now. Mom wants one

thing, Dad wants another. And she and Sherri are caught in the middle, powerless and scared.

She plays the chords again and suddenly she's singing. "Caught in the middle, between two dreams, that's how it seems—but I've got dreams, too."

Rae hears the doorknob turn. The door opens and Sherri peaks in. Rae keeps playing, so her sister slips inside and sits cross-legged on the floor, listening.

There are only two people in the world who have heard Rae's songs—Sherri and Luna. Both girls like them, but Rae doesn't put much stock in their opinions. Luna is her best friend, and Sherri—well, she's just her sister. Still, it feels good to see Sherri's body sway as Rae sings, "Caught in the middle, between two lives, I don't know who's right—but I want to live, too."

Suddenly the door opens again. Rae stops playing as Barrels comes bounding into the room. Then the door closes and she hears her mother's voice out in the hallway saying, "He can stay the week. Then he has to go."

Rae and Sherri grin at each other as Barrels hops on the bed. Sherri gets on, too, and she and the little dog curl up next to Rae. "Keep playing," Sherri whispers.

Rae strums her guitar and sings softly. The next time she looks, both Barrels and her sister are fast asleep.

6

*T*he next morning, Rae wakes up and wonders why her face tickles. She opens her eyes and sees a floppy dog ear brushing against her cheek. Barrels is sleeping next to her, and on his other side is Sherri, snoring softly.

Now the events of last night come rushing back— the horrible news of her parents' separation, the song she started to write, the sweet sight of Sherri and Barrels curled up on her bed. She can barely remember putting her guitar down and joining them. She must have been so exhausted she just passed out.

Rae reaches out to scratch Barrels. His eyes pop open and his tail thumps against the bed. Slowly, trying not to disturb Sherri, Rae sits up and wiggles her way down to the bottom of the bed. She slips on some clean clothes and walks into the hall. She hears a thump, and suddenly Barrels is beside her, prancing back and forth and looking ready for anything.

"Bet you're hungry," she says, walking into the kitchen.

"What?" Mom asks, looking up from the table. It's cluttered with papers, receipts, Mom's cell phone, a telephone book, and a half-empty coffee cup. Mom's still in her robe, her hair uncombed, a pencil behind her ear.

"What's all this?" Rae asks.

"It's time to start planning this year's Day at the Ranch. Can you believe it? This is our fifth year."

Rae isn't surprised. It feels as if Mom has always been in charge of the Crescent Cove Trail Riding Club's annual Day at the Ranch. She thought it up, in fact. It's a day when local kids who are battling cancer can come to Brandy Canyon Stables and forget their problems. There are horseback rides, pie-eating contests, games, and prizes. And thanks to the local ranchers and businessmen who volunteer their time and money, it's all free.

"It's going to be hard to pull off without your father's help," Mom says. "But life goes on, right?"

Mom doesn't look so sure, and Rae wonders how they'll manage without her father around. And it's not just the Day at the Ranch Rae is worried about. Dad was the one who balanced the checkbook and paid the bills, the one who knew how to fix practically anything, the one who could make Mom laugh when she was taking things too seriously—which was practically all the time. But Rae nods anyway because she knows Mom expects it.

"Did you sleep all right?" her mother asks.

Not really, Rae thinks, but decides not to say it. Then it occurs to her that she should thank her mother for allowing Barrels to sleep in her room. Usually Mom doesn't like dogs in the house, period. But before she can say anything, Mom asks, "What's that noise?"

There's a strange scratching sound coming from the living room. Rae walks into the room and blanches. Barrels looks like he's trying to dig a hole in the sofa! "Stop that!" Rae shouts. "Barrels, no!"

Mom appears just as Barrels grabs a throw pillow in his teeth and runs behind the love seat. "Oh, my Lord!" she cries. "Rae, get him out of here! I knew I shouldn't have bent my no-dogs-in-the-house rule."

Rae runs behind the love seat, but Barrels dashes away, still dragging the pillow. She chases him around the sofa, into the kitchen, and back into the living room. Finally she corners him in the coat closet and grabs him by the collar she put on him earlier. "Bad dog!" she scolds. He drops the pillow and she leads him outside.

Harley and Nipper appear from the stables and the

three dogs circle Rae, whining and begging for breakfast. "All right, all right!" she says. "Just relax."

She's pouring dog food into bowls—and wondering how the sweet little dog who slept next to her last night could have turned into such a hellion—when Mom walks out of the house carrying the portable phone.

"It's for you," she says. "A boy."

Rae's heart does an off-the-lip. Could it be? She lifts the receiver to her ear and stammers, "He-hello?"

"Hey, Rae, it's Shane. What's up?"

"My friends and I found a dog on the beach yesterday," she babbles. "If we can't find the owner, we're going to keep him. Only this morning—"

"That's cool," Shane breaks in. "Listen, some buddies and I are surfing at Luna Bay this morning—Trent Kalesworth, J. J. Bosco, a couple others. You wanna come?"

Trent Kalesworth? J. J. Bosco? They're both pro surfers. Of course she wants to come—although the thought of surfing with them makes her so nervous she can hardly breathe. "Hold on, Shane," she says, gulping.

She runs after Mom, who is heading back into the house. "Mom," she says, talking so fast the words run together, "can I go surfing before camp this morning?"

"I'm sorry, Rae, but the answer is no," Mom says flatly. "I'm leading a trail ride into Owl Creek Canyon in half an hour and I need you to come along."

"But why?" Rae wails.

"Things are changing, Rae. I told you that last night. Your father will still be helping us out financially, but it won't be like before. We've got to tighten our belts, and that means I'm going to rely on you to do a lot more around here—handle more chores, maybe even teach some lessons and lead some trail rides. You're old enough now."

"But this morning?" Rae moans. "How long is this ride anyway? I can't be late for surf camp."

"Truth be told, you might have to quit that job if it conflicts with your responsibilities around here."

It's all too much for Rae to deal with. So she concentrates on the most immediate problem. "I *will* help more around here, I promise. But can't I go surfing just this once? Please?"

"With that boy on the phone?" she asks skeptically. "Who is he?"

"Shane Fox. He's really nice, Mom. Please?"

"Shane Fox? The boy from your high school who dropped out to become a professional surfer? You know how I feel about that. The answer is no."

"Rae?" Shane is saying. "Rae, are you there?"

Rae gives her mother one last imploring look, but all she gets in return is stony silence. With a groan, she holds the phone to her ear and says, "I can't go."

"What? Why not?" Shane asks incredulously. Apparently he doesn't have to ask his mother for permission to go surfing. After all, it's his job.

"I'll tell you later." If there *is* a later, she thinks. Maybe after this Shane will decide she's too lame to bother with.

"Bye, Rae," he says and hangs up.

Rae hits the OFF button and flings the phone into the dirt.

"What are you doing?" Mom cries. "Pick that up this minute. And start saddling the horses. I'm going inside to wake up your sister."

Rae picks up the phone and drags herself into the stables. She puts a halter on Mandy, a chestnut Arabian, and leads her out to the corral. She's getting a saddle from the tack room when she hears barking. Oh, no! What now?

Rushing back to the corral, she finds Barrels running in circles around Mandy and yipping excitedly. She's wagging her tail, eager to play, but Mandy doesn't know that. She whinnies and stamps her front hoof. Barrels backs up and lunges at Mandy. The mare rises up on her hind legs. Barrels backs up again and lowers his head, ready to lunge.

"Barrels, no!" Rae screams.

Mom comes running out of the house again, this time with Sherri at her heels. "Oh, good heavens!" Mom cries. "Catch that dog and lock him in one of the stables—before someone gets hurt!"

Rae runs across the corral and grabs Barrels by the tail. When he spins around, she clutches his collar and drags him into the nearest stable.

When Rae returns, Mom is holding Mandy's halter and patting her neck. "That dog has got to go," Mom says. Her voice is subdued, but Rae knows that's only because she's trying to calm Mandy.

"But I promised to take care of him until the end of the week," Rae pleads. "Or until we find his owner."

Mom sighs. "Till the end of the week and that's it. But you have to keep him locked in the stables. Got it?"

Rae nods. "Got it."

The sound of a car coming up the driveway makes Mom's eyes grow wide. "Oh, dear Lord, it can't be the people for the trail ride already!"

Rae looks—and gasps. She recognizes that green Mercedes. It's Dad!

"Daddy!" Sherri squeals, running to meet him as he steps out of the car.

He catches her in his arms and hugs her tight. Rae runs up, too, and he leans down to kiss her head.

"I thought you were in Chicago," Sherri says.

"Not yet." He steps back and smiles broadly at his daughters. "Have you had breakfast yet, girls?"

"No," the girls respond in unison.

"Then let's go get some."

"Hang on a minute," Mom breaks in. "You can't just waltz in here and whisk the girls away whenever you feel like it. Besides, Rae is helping me lead a trail ride this morning."

Dad's face tightens. "They're my girls, too, Sara. Anyway, you've had a chance to explain what's going on between us. Now it's my turn."

Rae holds her breath. She's only been awake for half an hour, and already she's clashed with her mother over surfing, Shane, Barrels, *everything*. She's dying to get out of there and just chill. If she can't go surfing with Shane, breakfast with her dad is definitely the next best thing.

"All right," Mom says at last.

Rae and Sherri let out a cheer and hop into their father's car. Soon they're whizzing down Brandy Canyon Road on the way to their favorite breakfast place, Pancakes on the Pier. Dad makes small talk as they drive, questioning the girls about camp and their friends.

Rae tells him about Barrels's attack on the throw pillow, and his attempts to play chase with Mandy. Unlike Mom, Dad thinks the whole thing is hilarious. Rae smiles at her father. She loves his wavy red hair and sparkling blue eyes, the casual way he throws his arm over the steering wheel, the way he tosses his head back when he laughs. When Dad's around, life feels like an adventure.

They're sitting in the restaurant, chowing down on

stacks of blueberry pancakes and gazing out at the surf, when Dad says suddenly, "I leave for Chicago next week."

The syrupy pancakes stick in Rae's throat. "Why, Dad?" she asks. "Can't you just keep on working here?"

"My boss wants me to pump some life into the Midwest sales force," he explains. "It will probably be a short-term assignment, just until we get sales figures up again."

"But can't you say no?" Rae presses.

Dad grimaces. "It wouldn't be good to turn down something like this. With all the layoffs going on at the company, they might decide I'm not a team player and lay me off, too."

"But you'll be so far away," Sherri says. "When will we get to see you?"

"That's what I want to talk to you about." Dad takes a sip of his coffee, pauses, and then says cheerfully, "Why don't you both move to Chicago with me?"

"Chicago?" Rae sputters. "Just Sherri and me?"

"Why not? It's a great city, full of exciting things to do—world-class museums, incredible restaurants, all kinds of culture and diversity you won't find here in Crescent Cove."

"But you can't ride horses in downtown Chicago," Sherri points out.

"Or surf," Rae adds.

"You can take riding lessons outside of the city," Dad says. "And, Rae, there may not be an ocean, but there is Lake Michigan. How'd you like to learn to windsurf?"

Rae is speechless. Windsurf? It sounds fun, but what about her surfing career? Her friends? Shane? And what about Mom? She would completely freak if Rae and Sherri moved in with Dad, Rae's sure of it.

"Look, girls, I'm not asking you to decide right this minute," Dad says. "All I'm saying is think about it."

Rae glances at her sister. She looks just as confused as Rae feels. Rae frowns and pokes her pancakes with her fork. She's got a lot of thinking to do.

7

As they leave the restaurant, Dad asks, "Where to now, girls?"

"Home," Sherri answers. "Aileen and her mother are picking me up for riding camp."

Rae looks at her watch. Eight o'clock. Mom probably wants her home. But surf camp starts in an hour. If she goes home now, Mom will probably think up a bunch of chores for her and decide she shouldn't go to camp at all.

"I'm going to walk to the Beach Park," she says. "The girls are probably there by now. We'll hang out until surf camp starts."

"You sure you want to walk?" Dad asks. "I can drop you off."

"No, thanks. I need some time to think."

"That's my girl." He gives her a hug. "Have fun at camp. I'll call you tomorrow."

Rae loves that her father doesn't stress over stupid things, or ask a lot of annoying questions. If Mom were here, she'd be all over Rae. *Don't talk to strangers. If the girls aren't on the beach, walk up to Luna's house. How do I know you aren't sneaking off to meet that boy?*

But Dad just trusts her to take care of herself.

Rae waves as Dad and Sherri drive away. Then she leaves the pier and heads up the beach. Glancing at the surf, she remembers shooting the pier—and the sight of that piling coming at her. Scary! But exciting, too, and she wonders when she can try it again.

Not today. The surf is too slow and mushy. She thinks about Shane and wonders if he and his friends got any good waves. Probably not. Still, she would have given anything to go out with them.

Next time Shane asks her to surf, Rae vows, she won't even ask her mother. Why bother? Mom thinks Shane is some kind of juvenile delinquent just because he chose a surfing career over a high school diploma.

But will there even be a next time? Not if she and Sherri move to Chicago with Dad. She tries to imagine it. Where would they live? Where would she go to school? And most of all, how would she survive without surfing?

On the other hand, she wouldn't have to deal with

her mother's nonstop "surfers are slackers" rant. She wouldn't have to feed horses every evening, or smell horse manure when she woke up in the morning. And she wouldn't have to hear the disappointment in her mother's voice when she tells her friends, "Rae isn't much of a horsewoman. She'd rather surf than ride."

She walks on, trying to picture herself living in an apartment in the city, concrete and asphalt everywhere, taxis and buses whizzing by. Maybe she'd wear a uniform and go to some snooty prep school. She imagines wrapping a scarf around her neck and stepping out into the wind and snow to meet her friends—where? Not the beach, that's for sure.

Rae looks around at the blue sky, the glassy green ocean, the soft white sand beneath her feet. How could she ever leave this place? She loves it here.

Crescent Cove Beach Park is just ahead. Rae breaks into a run. She scrambles over the rocks at the north end of Luna Bay just in time to see Shane, Trent Kalesworth, and J. J. Bosco walk out of the water, surfboards under their arms. She stops and stares. She's seen Trent and J. J.'s photos in surfing magazines. On posters even! And now, here they are in the flesh!

At that moment, Shane spots her. *Oh, my gosh,* she thinks, *I'm standing here ogling them like some kind of groupie.* Quickly she smiles and walks over, trying to look casual and totally cool. "Hey, Shane," she calls.

"So you showed up after all," he says. "But where's your board?"

"I didn't bring it. I was eating breakfast on the pier with my dad."

"Oh," he says lightly, and Rae realizes he doesn't know her parents are breaking up, or even that they haven't been getting along.

There's so much we still have to learn about each other, she thinks, and suddenly it occurs to her that she's thinking about Shane not just as a mentor or a coach, but as a friend—or even something more.

The thought startles her, and she feels her cheeks heating up. She notices Trent and J. J. looking at her, which makes her blush even more.

"Hi," Trent says. "I'm Trent Kalesworth."

"I know," she blurts. "And you're J. J. Bosco. Number eight and number twelve on the tour."

They laugh. "Very good," J. J. says. "Do you know our shoe sizes and Social Security numbers, too?"

They laugh some more, and Rae feels like a total idiot. She looks to Shane for help, and to her great relief he says, "Speaking of standings, Rae came in second in the ASA Western Championship." Then he adds, "Girls' division, of course."

Now Rae doesn't know whether to be flattered or irritated. Shane tacked on "girls' division" as if that somehow made her second-place trophy less impressive. "I could beat most of the guys, too, if they'd give me a chance," she says.

"I'd like to see that," Trent chuckles.

"Maybe you will someday," Shane declares. He turns to his friends. "I told Rae that if she can prove to me she's ready, I'll give her some pointers."

Rae frowns. He makes it sound like she came to him begging for help. She wants to remind him that he was the one who asked her to go surfing, but then she decides against it. After all, she does think he has a lot to teach her. The rest of it doesn't really matter.

The guys start peeling off their wet suits. "You going to that surf clinic in Waikiki next month?" J. J. asks.

"Yeah," Shane replies. "I hate that rinky-dink stuff— I mean, half the kids who show up are tourists from the Midwest—but Edge wants me to make an appearance."

"At least we'll be able to get some good waves during the down time," Trent points out. "With luck, Ala Moana will be smoking."

Rae is hanging on every word. She's read about Hawaii's South Shore and its epic summer surf. How she'd love to see—and surf—it for herself!

"Does Makaha break on a south swell?" she asks, naming another famous Oahu surf break.

"It can, for sure," J. J. replies. "You've surfed it, haven't you, Trent?"

"That place is heavy, man. I got nailed on this one Godzilla-size wave. When I paddled in, Greg Noll was sitting there. He said, 'I know how you feel, kid.' "

Rae can hardly believe her ears. Greg Noll is one of the pioneers of surfing, and one of the best to ever ride Makaha. And J. J. met him!

"You mean he can still remember?" Shane snickers. "I mean, come on, the dude must be at least a hundred years old."

"Someday you'll be sitting here," Trent says, "and some young punk will walk by and say, 'Isn't that Shane Fox? Poor old geezer. He must be at least a hundred years old!' "

Everyone laughs, but Shane just shakes his head and says, "Not likely. My motto is live fast, die young, and leave a good-looking corpse."

As he speaks, he slips his arm around Rae's waist. She tenses, a flood of emotions washing over her. Can it be? Yes, he really does have his arm around her. But what does it mean? That he likes her? That he thinks of her as his girlfriend? She doesn't know. All she knows is that her brain is fogging over and her nervous system is short-circuiting.

"I gotta go take a shower," J. J. says, picking up his board. "I've got a photo shoot for Spider Sunglasses at eleven."

"This is my day off," Trent says. "I'm going back to bed."

"Later," Shane calls as they walk away.

"I can't believe I just met Trent Kalesworth and J. J. Bosco!" Rae exclaims after they've left. "They are such awesome surfers!"

"They better watch their backs," Shane says, "because I'm hot on their tails."

He has a look in his eye that reminds Rae of a shark—cold and deadly—and she has no doubt that he means what he says. It scares her a little, but it also makes her pulse race. Shane wants to win the pro surfing title, and he isn't going to stop until he does.

Do I have that kind of drive and desire? she wonders. She isn't sure, but she'd certainly like to find out.

"Uh-oh, I have to go," she says, noticing Luna's parents unloading surfboards from their van. "Surf camp is about to start."

"What do you need surf camp for?" he asks. "I'll teach you everything you need to know."

"It's run by Luna's parents. I'm an assistant counselor. It's fun. All the little kids think we're hot stuff."

"You *are* hot stuff," he says, pulling her so close that his nose is almost touching hers. Rae can feel his warm breath on her chin and his arms encircling her waist. She feels as if her muscles are melting, and she wonders how she's managing to remain vertical.

"I think we should start spending time together," he says.

"Okay," she breathes, staring into his pale blue eyes.

"I can teach you a lot."

She nods, trancelike.

"Besides, my arms fit around you just right."

"Uh-huh."

Shane's arms drop from her waist. He steps back and picks up his board. "There's a big west swell coming in. I'm going up to Palos Verdes with Trent and J. J. tomorrow."

"I wish I could go." Rae sighs.

He shrugs. "It might be a little out of your league. When Lower Trestles is cranking, the big boys come out to play. And they don't like to share."

Is Shane right? Is Lower Trestles too heavy for her? She's always thought she could handle anything. But now she's not so sure.

"Call me when you get back, okay?" she says.

He touches her cheek and whispers, "You can count on it."

Then he walks away, leaving Rae to stagger toward surf camp on limp, lovestruck legs.

Mom, please," Rae begs as her mother drives down Brandy Canyon Road, "just give him one more chance." She lifts Barrels's furry head off the seat. "Look at that face. How can you say no?"

"Just watch me," Mom replies.

Rae can't believe her mother can be so cruel. "You have a heart of stone," she tells her.

"That's unfair," Mom says. "That dog almost destroyed my sofa, frightened my horses, dug up my lawn, and knocked over one of my riding students."

"The girl was holding a ham sandwich less than a foot over Barrels's head," Rae replies. "He couldn't help himself."

"If you had kept him locked in the stables the way I asked you to—"

"So I forgot to put on the lock one time. Everybody makes mistakes."

Mom sighs. "I'm sorry, Rae. I let him stay for three days, but that's it. Now it's Luna's turn."

Rae pats Barrel's furry head. "I'm going to miss you, boy," she says sadly.

"Where's the owner?" Mom wonders aloud as she turns down Surf Street. "Are you sure you put up enough posters?"

Rae nods. "And we put an ad in the *Crescent Cove Reporter,* too."

"If you ask me, Barrels's owner is happy to pass him on to a new victim. That pooch is trouble."

Mom pulls up in front of the Shoreline Surf Shop. Rae grabs her guitar from the backseat and hops out. Barrels is right behind her. "Can I sleep over?" Rae asks.

"Not tonight. I want you home by nine. Tomorrow's Saturday and I have lessons and trail rides all day."

"Oh, no," Rae groans, assuming she's expected to help out.

But her mother surprises her by saying, "While I'm working, I need you and Sherri to clean the house."

"What? Where's Lucinda?" Lucinda has been coming twice a month to clean the Perraults' house for as long as Rae can remember.

"I had to let her go," Mom says. "Paying someone to clean my house is a luxury I can't afford right now."

Rae can't believe it. Since her parents' split, life with Mom has become absolute torture. All she does is worry about money and think up chores for Rae and Sherri to do.

No one would believe that Mom used to criticize Dad for fretting over money, Rae thinks. *Now she's turned into a worse miser than he ever was.*

Turning her back on her mother and her troubles, Rae walks into the surf shop. Barrels scampers in after her. Luna's dad, Tuck, is behind the counter. Her mother, Cate, is showing a surfboard to a customer.

"Hey, Rae," Tuck says, lifting his bottle of ice tea. "Here's to a successful first week of beginners' surf camp."

Rae smiles. "I didn't think we'd ever get some of those kids standing on a surfboard. But we did."

"So this is the famous Barrels," Cate says, pausing from her sales pitch long enough to lean down and scratch him. "He's a cutie. Hard to believe his owner hasn't shown up."

Apparently Luna hasn't told her parents about Barrels's bad behavior. Rae decides not to enlighten them. "He's a great dog," she says.

"Luna's in the storeroom with Kanani," Tuck says. "Go on back."

Rae calls Barrels and they walk into the storeroom at the back of the shop. Luna and Kanani are there, putting price tags on board shorts.

"Big news!" Kanani exclaims as Rae walks in. "There's a big longboarding contest in Florida next month and Tuck and Cate said they'd take us!"

"Who's us?" Rae asks with interest.

"The girls! All of us who want to go. It's at Sebastian Inlet. I've always wanted to surf there. I mean, it's not Hawaii, but still . . . wow!"

Kanani was born in Hawaii, but she's lived in Crescent Cove with her adoptive parents since she was a baby. She's got a great life—she'd be the first to admit it—but she still longs to return to Hawaii and surf big island waves.

Luna pats her lap and Barrels jumps up. "We have to get our parents' permission," she explains as he licks her face, "and come up with enough money for a plane ticket. We're going to camp out and cook our own food. Do you think you can come, Rae?"

Rae snorts a laugh. "Not a chance. Ever since my parents split, my mother has turned into the world's worst penny-pincher. Besides, you know my mom barely tolerates me surfing right here. She's not going to send me to a contest in Florida."

"Bummer," Kanani declares.

"Unless . . ." Rae says thoughtfully.

"Unless what?" Luna asks.

"Unless I move to Chicago."

"*What?*" Kanani and Luna cry in unison.

Rae shrugs. "I told you my dad wants Sherri and me to move there. If I did, I bet you anything he'd pay for me to go with you guys. Unlike Mom, he actually supports my surfing."

"I know, but think about it, Rae," Luna argues. "I mean, the Florida trip will be a blast, no doubt about it. But when it's over, you'll still be living in Chicago."

Undeniably true, Rae tells herself. *And not a pretty picture.*

Then, suddenly, she has a revelation. "If I really hate it, I can always tell him I want to move back, right?"

"Hey," Luna says suddenly, "where's Barrels?"

"I thought he was on your lap," Kanani replies with a frown.

"He was, but he jumped off a couple of minutes ago. I was too busy talking to think about—"

Rae, who has seen the havoc Barrels is capable of, is on her feet. "We've got to find him. Come on."

They run into the shop. "Split up," she tells her friends. "Kanani, you go left. Luna, right. I'll take the middle."

Rae weaves through the clothing racks and display cases, looking for Barrels. Suddenly she hears Luna's sinking, "Oh, no!" She follows her friend's voice and finds Barrels gnawing on a shrink-wrapped boogie board. He's already managed to rip off the plastic and shred one corner.

"Bad dog!" Rae shouts, pulling the board out of his mouth.

"That's not a cheap board, either," Luna says anxiously. "It's a Mike Stewart model, top of the line."

Tuck, Cate, and Kanani appear a moment later. "Are you telling me the dog did that?" Cate cries.

Rae and Luna nod.

"You've got to be kidding!" Tuck practically screams. "That's like a two-hundred-dollar board, and it's ruined."

"Take that dog into the backyard," Cate orders. She looks at Tuck. "What have we gotten ourselves into?"

Rae looks at Barrels and wonders the same thing.

"Caught in the middle, between two dreams, that's how it seems—but I've got dreams, too," Rae sings as she strums her guitar.

It's later that evening, and she's sitting on the beach with Luna and Kanani. Barrels is running in and out of the water, chasing birds and playing tag with the other dogs.

"Caught in the middle, between two lives, I don't know who's right—but I want to live, too." Rae strums the final chord and looks up shyly.

"I love that," Kanani says without hesitation.

"Really?" Rae asks uncertainly.

Kanani nods, and Luna says, "You already know I love your singing and guitar playing. But honestly, Rae, your writing is getting better with each song. This new one is so personal, so real. It just blows me away."

Rae knows she's grinning like a fool, but she can't help it. She still can't quite think of herself as a song-writer. But if Luna and Kanani think she's good, well, maybe she should keep at it.

"I was in Java Jones yesterday," Kanani says, "and there was a poster up advertising their Open Mike Night. You ought to play there, Rae."

"In public?" she says incredulously. "I don't think so."

"Why not?" Luna asks. "You've got talent. Why not share it?"

Rae considers. Would she have the courage to get up in front of all those people and sing her songs? Just the thought of it makes her mouth go dry.

"Maybe someday," she mutters.

"We'll come and support you," Kanani insists. "Isobel and Cricket, too. Come on, Rae. This could be the start of a new career."

Rae laughs. She'd like to get her surfing career going first. Then, after she wins her first world title, she'll put out a CD and—

Her fantasy is cut short by Barrels, who has decided to dig a hole right next to them. His short little legs are kicking sand right into the girls' faces.

"Hey, stop that!" Luna cries.

Barrels stops, puts his front paws on Luna's shoulders, and barks in her face.

"What is the matter with this dog?" Luna asks, holding her ears.

"He's a high-energy mutt," Rae replies. "If you don't keep him moving, he gets into trouble. Believe me, I know."

"Let's take him for a walk," Kanani suggests.

"You two go ahead," Rae says. "I'm going to stay here and play some music."

Luna and Kanani stand up. Barrels runs in circles around them, barking joyously. "Race you to the pier!" Luna shouts, breaking into a run. Barrels dashes after her, with Kanani bringing up the rear.

Rae watches them go, then turns her attention to her guitar. She's trying to write a song about surfing, but it's so hard to get the lyrics right. How can she put into words the way it feels to drop down the face of a perfect head-high wave?

"My blue mountain," she sings. "A cliff of moving water, I can't name you, can't try to tame you . . ."

"Whoo-ooo-ooo," a whiny voice wails.

Rae spins around and sees Shane standing behind her, his head thrown back like a coyote howling at the moon. "Don't stop," he says in a fake Southern accent. "I'm just providing a little harmony." He tosses back his head again. "Whoo-ooo-ooo!"

"Stop it." Rae giggles, not sure whether to be amused or offended.

Shane laughs and sits down facing her. "I didn't know you played the guitar."

"Kind of," she admits. "Hey, how was your trip down south?"

"Epic! Lower Trestles was double overhead." He nods at her guitar. "Go on, sing something."

"No," she says with a bashful shrug. "I'm not that good. I was just fooling around."

"Please." He leans closer and puts his chin on her shoulder. "I'd really like to hear you."

"Well . . . okay. If you promise not to laugh."

"I promise," he replies, crossing his heart. He sits up and gazes at her attentively. "Go ahead."

Rae sings the song about her parents' separation, the one she just sang for Luna and Kanani. When the last chord dies away, she takes a deep breath and looks up. Shane looks back, saying nothing.

"Well?" Rae stammers, wiping her sweaty palms on her shorts.

"Nice," Shane says at last.

Nice? Rae doesn't know what to think. Is he talking about her voice, her playing, the music, the lyrics? None of them are especially nice, in her opinion. Intense, maybe. Deep. Sincere. But *nice*? That's almost an insult.

"Luna and Kanani think I should perform at the Open Mike Night at Java Jones," she says defensively.

Brow furrowed, Shane hesitates. "Rae, I—I'm only saying this because I really care about you. The people who perform at Java Jones aren't amateurs—even the ones who play at Open Mike Night. I mean, some of them have CDs out." He looks pained. "Maybe you should wait awhile, keep practicing. I'll let you know when you're ready."

With Shane's words, Rae's confidence slips like a hillside house in a mudslide. Her shoulders slump and her smile turns inside out. But Shane hugs her tight and says, "You want to know my theory?"

She nods into his shoulder.

He holds her hands and looks her in the eye. "Everyone has lots of talents. But each individual has only one thing—only one—that he was born to do. The sad thing is, some people never figure out what it is. But if you're lucky enough to find your special talent, you'd be a fool not to go all the way with it."

"You mean surfing?" Rae says tentatively.

Shane nods. "You're like me, Rae. You were born to ride waves."

"You really think so?"

"I know it. And you owe it to yourself to develop your talent to the limit. If you have to lose friends, drop out of school, leave home . . . whatever it takes, *do* it. It will be worth it in the long run, I can promise you that."

Rae looks into Shane's fiery eyes. She can feel their heat warming her face, her heart, her very soul. He leans closer . . . closer . . .

Then he kisses her and the whole world explodes.

9

*H*a!" Sherri cries, bursting into Rae's room like the secret police. "You're busted! Just wait till I tell Mom . . ."

"Hold on!" Rae calls, jumping up from her computer. "I was cleaning my room—honest. I just stopped to check out this website. It's about Chicago."

Sherri stops and turns back. "Yeah?"

"It's got information, photos, all kinds of stuff. It's even got the weather report. Guess what the temperature is in downtown Chicago right now?"

"What?"

"Ninety-eight. You could cook an omelet on the sidewalk."

Sherri looks out the window. The sun is shining and a light breeze is rustling the tree leaves. The temperature is about seventy-five.

Rae looks, too. Somewhere out there her mother is taking a group of tourists on a trail ride. When she returns, she'll expect to see the house looking as clean and orderly as it does when Lucinda leaves.

"I'll pay you a dollar to clean the hall bathroom for me," Rae offers.

"No way," Sherri answers. "I'm doing the master bathroom, you're doing the hall one. We agreed."

"Come on, shrimp," Rae says. "You don't want me to have to tell Mom that you're the one who broke her crystal horse figurine."

"Go ahead. But then I'll have to tell her that you were hanging out on the beach with Shane Fox last night."

"How do know that?" Rae demands.

"I heard you talking on the phone to Isobel." Sherri walks over and looks at the computer screen. "Do they have any photos of wintertime in Chicago?"

"Yep." She clicks on the photo icon and brings up a photograph of downtown Chicago during a blizzard. Pedestrians in heavy coats and hats are struggling to walk as high winds blow snow into their faces.

"Ew," Sherri squeaks with a shiver.

"I did find one interesting photo, though," Rae admits. She clicks her mouse, and up pops a photo of a windsurfer roaring across Lake Michigan.

"I could see you doing that," Sherri says with a smile.

"Me, too. But what about the other ten months of the year?"

Sherri plops herself on Rae's bed. "Did Dad call you yesterday?"

Rae nods.

"Me, too. He asked if I'd thought any more about moving to Chicago with him. I didn't know what to say. What did you say, Rae?"

"I asked him what Mom thought about it. He said he hadn't talked to her yet. Sherri, she's going to go ballistic."

Sherri looks worried. Rae knows how she feels. Just thinking about her parents' split makes her stomach hurt.

The phone rings. Eager to change the subject, Rae jumps to answer it. It's Luna, and she doesn't sound happy. "Hold on a sec," Rae says, covering the receiver and turning to her sister. "Clean the hall bathroom for me and I'll take you surfing."

Sherri's eyes light up. "And give me a lesson, too?"

Rae nods.

"When?" asks Sherri.

"Tomorrow."

Sherri grins. "Deal."

Rae watches her sister leave, then says into the phone, "What's up?"

"This morning Barrels got into the surf wax," Luna

announces. "He ate about five bars and then threw up all over my parents' bed."

"Uh-oh." Rae gulps.

"Yeah, they were not happy. In fact, they said Barrels has to go. I'm taking him over to Kanani's house this afternoon."

Rae sighs. "How can that dog be so adorable and so impossible at the same time?"

"Kind of like boys." Luna laughs and launches into a long story about how David wouldn't go to the mall with her because he wanted to watch an Anaheim Angels game on TV. "Like he couldn't tape it?" she exclaims. "Come on!"

Rae knows her friend wants someone to commiserate with, but right now she has nothing bad to say about boys. She thinks about Shane—his pale blue eyes and killer smile—and her heart skips a beat. But there's no point in talking about Shane to Luna. She still thinks he's a boastful brat.

She doesn't know the real Shane, Rae thinks with a blissful smile.

Rae has barely hung up when the phone rings again. "It's me," says Cricket, her words flying through the phone lines like machine-gun fire. "Guess what? Remember Blaine Barker, that photographer I introduced you to at the Championship—the one who photographed my dad at Carson Beach?"

Cricket's father, Chet Connolly, has been surfing Malibu since the sixties. He's a legend to a lot of surfers, not just for his surfing ability, but because he's an eccentric maverick who shuns contests, sponsors, and crowded waves. Cricket hasn't seen him in person since he and her mom split ten years ago, but she keeps up with him through the newspapers and Barker's pictures.

Cricket is still talking, barely pausing long enough to take a breath. "And remember how he said he wanted to photograph a surf session with the five of us? Well, he called and wants to do it tomorrow. There's supposed to be a southwest swell coming in so I suggested Carson Beach and he said okay. I already called Isobel, Kanani, and Luna. They're all gonna be there. Seven o'clock sharp. Can you come, Rae?"

Rae laughs. She loves Cricket's energy, although sometimes she wonders about her motivation for surfing. Cricket pretends she couldn't care less about her dad, but when he didn't show up to see her surf the Championship, it was obvious she was disappointed. Is she hoping a photo spread in a magazine might convince him to contact her?

Rae doesn't know if she should ask. In any case, she has her own reasons for wanting to make the surf session. Blaine Barker's photographs regularly appear in national surf magazines.

If my photo got published, she thinks, *it could really help my career.*

"Sure, I'll be there," she says eagerly.

Rae hangs up and thinks how pleased Shane will be when she tells him. He wants her to get serious about her career. Well, what better way than by getting her photo in a well-respected mag?

"Rae," Sherri says, appearing breathless in the doorway, "guess what?"

"The toilet overflowed?" Rae asks.

"No. Shane 'The Pain' Fox is here to see you."

Rae practically levitates off the chair. In a panic, she throws off her T-shirt and sweatpants and puts on a cotton blouse and shorts. She combs her hair, slathers lip gloss across her mouth, and walks with studied casualness into the living room.

Shane is sitting on the sofa, glancing through the *Horses of the World* book. "Hey there," he says.

"Hey there."

Shane grins. "You said you lived on a ranch, so I thought I'd come by and see for myself."

Sherri is standing in the dining room, watching them with interest. "Yep, we're a couple of real cowgirls," she snickers. "Rae can shoot a rattlesnake right between the eyes with her rifle."

Rae glares at her threateningly. "*Two* surf lessons—if you get lost," she hisses.

"And a smoothie afterward."

"Okay, whatever. Just go!"

Sherri makes a quick exit, and Rae says, "Would you like to see the stables?"

"Sure."

They walk outside and across the corral. "There aren't too many horses around right now. My mom's leading a trail ride."

"Can we go riding, too?" Shane asks.

Rae hesitates. Her mother doesn't like beginners to ride the horses unless she's with them. Plus, she makes everyone sign a waiver saying that if they get hurt, Brandy Canyon Stables isn't responsible.

"Come on, cowgirl," Shane urges, kissing her lightly on the nose. "Please?"

How can she say no to that? She saddles two of the horses—Silver for Shane and Moose for her—and gives Shane a quick lesson in mounting and riding. Then they climb on and walk the horses around the corral.

"This is getting boring," he says after their second time around. "Let's hit the trail."

"Okay, but we can't go far. My mother doesn't like me to take the horses out without her permission. If she comes back and finds us—"

"She won't," he says confidently.

Rae leads the way. They walk around the house and

onto a little-used trail. It's a bit rocky, but at least she knows she won't run into her mother here.

"Rae, I've been thinking," Shane says as they ride. "I'm going to introduce you to my sponsors. They won't want to sign you now—after all, you've only been in one major contest—but it never hurts to start building relationships."

"Wow, thanks," she exclaims. "I know you're sponsored by Edge Surfwear, but are there others?"

"Sure. Spider Sunglasses, Traction Sandals, and Goldie's Surf Wax."

Rae is so impressed she can barely speak. Shane is so cool—and so generous, too. She glances over at him. The sunlight is behind him, making his hair look like a halo, and suddenly she finds herself wondering why she was so down on horseback riding. With Shane by her side, she could ride forever. Except—

"We'd better turn around," she says. "My mother will be back soon."

As they head back, Shane says, "Let's go faster. What's it called—trotting? Galloping?"

"Trotting comes next, but we'd better save that for another lesson."

"Oh, come on, Rae. What's the big deal?" He shakes the reins and leans forward. "Let's go, Silver! Charge!"

The horse breaks into a bumpy trot. Shane lets out a surprised yelp as he bounces forward.

"Sit back!" Rae calls. "Pull on the reins!"

Instead, he leans forward and grabs Silver's mane to steady himself. With an eager snort, the horse breaks into a canter.

Rae stares in shock at Shane's receding figure. What if he falls off? Or runs into something? Quickly, she urges her own horse into a canter. "Shane," she calls, "don't panic. I'm coming!"

She can hear the beating of Silver's hooves up ahead on the trail, but she can't see him. With her heart pounding, she rounds the final bend just in time to see Mom and three tourists walking around the tack shed. And there's Shane—galloping right at them!

10

*R*ae's mother looks up at the horse and rider barreling toward her and gasps. The three women shriek and run in three different directions. Then Mom takes a step forward, holds up her hands, and says in a loud, firm voice, "Silver, whoa!"

To Rae's amazement, the horse comes to an abrupt stop, nearly causing Shane to fly over its head. Unbelievably, Shane does manage to stay on, but he's left hanging off Silver's side with both feet dangling and his hands clutching the horse's neck in a death grip. If Rae wasn't so freaked, she'd laugh. He looks ridiculous!

Instead, it's Shane who laughs as he drops to the ground. "That was trippy!" he cries as Rae trots her horse over. "When can we do it again?"

Rae is speechless, but her mother isn't. "Rae Ann Perrault," she snaps, her eyes shooting sparks, "what is going on here?"

"Mom," Rae stammers, getting off her horse, "uh, this is Shane. Shane, this is my mother."

"Hi," he says cheerfully, jumping to his feet.

Mom ignores him. "Number one, you are supposed to be cleaning the house," she tells Rae, counting on her fingers. "Two, you are not allowed to have boys in the house when I'm not there. And three, you are not allowed to take anyone riding without my permission."

"Hey, come on, it's not Rae's fault," Shane breaks in. "I mean, I showed up, so she decided to take a break, that's all. And then we went for a little ride. No big deal, right?"

Rae is torn between delight at the fact that Shane is trying to defend her and horror at the nonchalant way he's talking to her mother. Not surprisingly, Mom looks ready to explode. But before she can completely lose it, one of the three women who ran away reappears around the corner of the tack shed. Her clothes are dusty and her cowboy hat is askew.

"Is . . . is everything all right?" she asks in a shaky voice.

"Yes, yes," Mom says lightly, turning from Rae and Shane. "One of the horses got a little frisky, that's all. I'm sorry if he startled you."

The other two women peek around the house, their faces pale. "If you're sure . . ." one of them says.

"Absolutely. Listen, let me walk you to your cars. I want to give each of you a coupon for a half-price sunset beach ride."

"Hey, don't I get a coupon?" Shane asks. "I mean, I'm the one your crazy horse decided to take on a joyride."

Rae's mother turns on him. "High school dropouts are not welcome at this house," she hisses just loud enough for Shane and Rae to hear. "Especially not ones with smart mouths. Now please leave, and don't come back!"

Mom strides away and Shane turns to Rae with a "what's-her-problem?" look on his face. Rae looks down at her shoes. She wishes she could dig a hole and crawl in it. Okay, so maybe Shane *was* a little rude, but Mom didn't have to act so weird, did she? And that crack about high school dropouts was just too embarrassing.

"I'm sorry," Rae says weakly. "I told you my mom doesn't like me riding without her permission."

"Yeah, but come on!" he scoffs. "She was totally over the top. And what was that crack about high school dropouts?"

"She knows you dropped out of school to join the pro tour. She doesn't want me to do the same thing."

"Just for the record, I know dropping out wasn't the

smartest thing I ever did, so I took the GEDs and got a high school equivalency diploma. But hey, that's me. If I were you, I'd be out of this house so fast her head would spin." He laughs, then slips his arm around Rae's waist and pulls her close. "Come on, let's go surfing."

Is Shane kidding? "I can't," she says. "I'm probably grounded for like the next five years."

She tries to laugh, but Shane shakes his head disdainfully. "Whatever. I'm out of here."

He drops his arm and starts walking toward the driveway. "Wait," she pleads, hurrying after him. "Call me, okay?"

"Sure," he replies, but from the look on his face she can tell he won't.

Rae's heart sinks. She doesn't want to lose Shane. Not now, when so many other things seem to be going wrong. Frantically, she searches her mind for something to say, something that will keep him interested.

"Have you ever heard of Blaine Barker?" she asks.

He pauses. "The photographer?"

"That's right. My friend Cricket knows him. He asked a few of my friends and me to meet him at Carson Beach tomorrow for an early-morning surf session. He's going to photograph us, maybe even get us into one of the magazines. Do—do you want to come?"

She doesn't mention that all the friends Cricket

invited are girls, or that they might not appreciate having Shane show up. She hesitates, wondering if she was wrong to invite him. Then she sees the grin on his face, and she refiles her doubts in the part of her brain labeled LATER.

"I'll be there," he says. "I'm stoked."

Rae's heart takes flight. "Seven o'clock, okay? I'll meet you at the bottom of the stairs."

He leans in close to kiss her, then notices Rae's mom standing beside one of the tourist ladies' cars, glowering at him. He gives Mom a little wave and snickers. Then he gets in his jeep and drives away.

Rae hurries into the house, hoping to avoid Mom as long as possible. Instead, she meets Sherri. "You are so dead," she says, looking slightly awed.

"Oh, she'll get over it," Rae replies, trying to convince herself. She plops down on the sofa. "I'll do an extra-good job on the house cleaning and—"

"How could you do that to me?"

It's Mom. And to Rae's chagrin, she doesn't look so much mad as she does hurt. "What do you mean?" Rae asks.

Mom faces her across the coffee table. "How do you think those women felt seeing an out-of-control horse coming at them? Do you think they're going to want to ride here again? Or recommend me to their friends?"

Rae knows the answer. "But I bet they were

impressed with the way you made Silver stop on a dime," she says, reaching for something—anything—to make her mother lighten up. "I sure was."

Mom is barely listening. "It makes the stables look bad. It makes *me* look bad."

"I'm sorry, Mom. I was just—"

"How many times do I need to tell you? Money is tight right now. I need all the business I can get. And I need you girls to help me. Look at Sherri," Mom says, gesturing toward her. "She isn't causing trouble. She's cleaning the house just the way I asked her to. But you—"

Rae can't stand it. Sherri has always been the good one, the one her mother loves best. She glances at her sister, who is standing there with a can of cleanser in her hand and an innocent expression on her face. Rae scowls. She'd like to smack her with a toilet brush.

Instead, she jumps to her feet and glares at her mother. "What about *you*?" she blurts out. "You embarrassed me in front of my boyfriend."

"Boyfriend?" Mom gasps.

"He's not what you think he is, Mom. He's an awesome surfer, a sweet guy, and . . . and I love him!"

Rae isn't sure where that last part—the love part—came from. Does she really love Shane? She's not sure, but now that she's said it, she's not about to take it back.

Mom looks completely flabbergasted. "Love?" she sputters. "You don't know the meaning of the word."

"Look who's talking," Rae shoots back. "Your marriage is over, in case you didn't notice."

Mom looks as if Rae just slammed her in the stomach with a two-by-four. "You, young lady, are banned from the beach. No more surfing, no more working at surf camp!"

Now it's Rae who's flabbergasted. "*What?* Why?"

"It's obvious the people you've been spending time with are a bad influence," her mother says coldly. "Besides, you're going to be much too busy to surf. Starting today, I'm putting you in charge of feeding the horses every morning and evening. I also expect you to help me with all my trail and beach rides."

"That is so unfair! Surfing is my life! Don't you care about my feelings at all?"

Mom is unyielding. "If you want to ride something, Rae Ann, ride a horse."

"And what about Sherri? She just gets to sit around and watch TV?"

"Sherri is too young to lead trail rides," Mom snaps, "but she's helping out in plenty of other ways. Now go to your room and think about what I said. When you feel like being cooperative, you can come out and help your sister clean the house."

Mom points her finger down the hall. Rae jumps up, gives the coffee table an angry kick, and stomps to her room. She slams the door behind her and plops down in front of her computer. With a disgusted sigh, she taps the ENTER key. The photo of the Lake Michigan windsurfer reappears on the screen.

Rae stares at it, trying to picture herself flying across Lake Michigan's dark, choppy water. Why not? She could get into it. She'd probably be a terrific windsurfer, too. At least she'd be far away from Mom and her insane ideas. Dad wouldn't flip out just because she wanted to surf—oops, windsurf—with her boyfriend. Rae hears a tap on the door and turns around. A slip of paper slides under the door jam. She walks over and picks it up. The handwriting is Sherri's.

I'm sorry about what happened, it says. *And I'm really sorry we can't go surfing together tomorrow.*

Suddenly Rae doesn't feel so angry. Just depressed. Could anything more possibly go wrong? She doesn't think so.

Then, like a kick in the ribs, she realizes it already has. Not only can't she take Sherri surfing tomorrow, she can't go to the surf session at Carson Beach either.

My girlfriends are probably going to get their photos in a national surfing magazine, she thinks unhappily. *Shane, too. But not me.*

With a shuddering sigh, Rae walks over to her guitar and picks it up. There's a new song inside her, struggling to get out. She doesn't know the chords yet, or even the words. But she does know the title.

It's called "I Hate My Life."

11

*R*ae leans down and whispers in her horse's ear, "Moose, are you as bored as I am?"

Moose lifts his ears, and Rae figures that's a yes. They're walking at a snail's pace up Crescent Cove Beach behind Rae's mom and five beginning riders— a father, mother, and their three preteen children. How could he *not* be bored?

"Look, everyone," Rae's mother calls out, "dolphins!"

The five horseback riders spin their heads toward the ocean. At that very moment, three dolphins leap out of the water.

"Oh!" the mother gasps. The children squeal with delight.

"You can't see *that* in Des Moines!" the father says with a nod of satisfaction.

Rae sighs. The sight of leaping dolphins normally makes her heart sing. But today she just can't get excited. All she can think about are her friends—Luna, Kanani, Isobel, and Cricket—ripping at Carson Beach while Blaine Barker stands on the shore, snapping award-winning photos.

And Shane—did he show up, too? What did he think when he walked to the bottom of the beach stairs and Rae wasn't there? Did he leave in disgust? Or did he connect with Blaine and the girls and join their surf session?

Suddenly Rae has a dreadful thought. What if Shane is connecting a little too well—like what if he decides one of her girlfriends is more interesting than her? Not that any of her crew would be mean enough to flirt with Shane. In fact, she's pretty sure none of them even wants to. Still . . .

One of the children, a freckle-faced girl who looks about ten, turns in her saddle and grins at Rae. "You are so lucky," she says. "You get to ride your horse on the beach whenever you want."

Rae smiles back and nods. But to herself she's thinking, *Lucky?*

She gazes toward Luna Bay. Perfect four-foot waves are rolling in, and on every one, a surfer is shredding.

"Have you ever tried that?" she asks the girl, pointing as a surfer carves across the face of a wave.

"It looks scary," the girl says.

"No way," Rae says emphatically. "It's the ultimate rush!"

"Better than galloping across the beach on your very own horse?"

"Way better." Rae notices Mom glancing back at her. Uh-oh, no way she wants to get her mother mad at her again. "But this is fun, too," she adds.

They amble on, past North Beach, until they reach the pier. They get off the horses and Mom tells the family, "Time for lunch. If you want to explore the pier for about fifteen or twenty minutes while I set up, that would be fine."

The kids run ahead while their mother and father stroll along, hand in hand. Mom and Rae unpack food and drinks from the saddlebags. Mom spreads a tablecloth on the sand and Rae sets out the plates.

"Thanks for your help," Mom says with a smile. "These rides are much easier when you're along."

Rae can tell her mother is trying to make up, but she's not interested. She grunts noncommittally and turns toward the pier. Surfers are blasting down five-foot walls of water and shooting through the pilings. Rae remembers when she took that ride. The fear she felt is a distant memory, and now all she can think is, *What a rush!*

"Moose is too big a horse for you, Rae," Mom continues. "I'd like to see you on Dancer. She's got such a smooth canter. And fast! You could fly down the beach on her."

"I can't fly with these beginners around," Rae grumps.

"There are other times to ride," Mom replies. "I don't think I have anything scheduled for tomorrow morning. We could bring our favorite horses to the beach and ride together."

"No, thanks."

"But why, sweetie? I'd like to spend some time with you."

Rae feels a pang of guilt. Mom looks so eager, so hopeful. But then Rae remembers how her mother insulted Shane, forced her to quit surf camp, and banned her from doing the one thing in life that makes her truly happy.

"Well, I don't want to spend time with you," she mutters, turning away.

The parents and their kids pick that moment to return. Mom is all smiles now, passing out the sand-wiches and relating the history of Crescent Cove pier. But her eyes tell a different story, and Rae knows Mom is hurting.

Good, Rae thinks meanly. *Now you know how it feels.*

• • •

Later, back at the parking lot, Rae sees Luna, Kanani, Isobel, and Cricket eating lunch on the beach with the surf camp kids. Barrels is nearby, happily gnawing on a stick.

Rae's heart aches to watch her friends laughing and talking together—probably about their hot surf session with Blaine Barker this morning. If only she were with them!

Rae helps her mother load the horses into the trailer, but she can't stop glancing over her shoulder. The surf camp kids are finishing their lunches, grabbing their boards, and heading back into the waves. Rae thinks back to the first day of camp and how bored and impatient she was with the beginning surfers. Now she'd give anything to be paddling out with them.

Finally, she can't stand it anymore. "Mom," she says, "I need to talk to Luna for a minute. I—I left my watch at her house the last time I slept over."

The watch is right there on Rae's arm, but fortunately Mom doesn't notice. "Come right back," she says. "I'm almost ready to leave."

Rae runs down to the water's edge where her friends are kneeling together, waxing their boards. Barrels bounds up to meet her, his tail wagging. She drops down to hug him. "Hi, boy! Whose house are you staying at this week?"

"Mine," Kanani says, "but not for long. My mother

was defrosting a steak on the counter and he jumped up and ate it."

"The whole thing?" Rae asks incredulously.

Kanani nods. "It was still frozen, too."

"Where were you this morning, Rae?" Cricket asks.

"My mom banned me from surfing," she answers glumly. "Surf camp, too."

"What?" Luna gasps. "My parents said your Mom called and told them you couldn't come today, but I thought it was a one-time thing."

"I wish."

"What happened?" Isobel asks.

"Shane came over and we went horseback riding without permission," Rae explains. "Mom went nuts and made him leave." She frowns, remembering. "I expected a punishment, but not this. I can't see Shane, can't surf. It's torture!"

"We saw Shane," Kanani says quietly.

Rae spins to face her. "You did? Was he at Carson Beach this morning?"

"How did you know?" Kanani asks.

"I told him to meet me there," Rae replies.

"Did you tell him that Blaine Barker would be photographing us?" Cricket asks, her eyes narrowing as she chomps a wad of bubble gum.

"Sure," she says, then hesitates. Her friends are looking at her oddly, and suddenly she gets that same feeling she got yesterday, right after she invited Shane. Like maybe she'd spoken when she shouldn't have. Like maybe Shane wouldn't be welcome.

"He brought a couple of his pro buddies—Trent Kalesworth and J. J. Bosco," Luna says.

"I met them!" Rae breaks in eagerly, but quickly falls silent under her friends' disapproving glares.

"They were hot-dogging like crazy," Luna continues, "trying to outdo us. Like if one of us caught air, they'd take off on the very next wave and catch bigger air."

"They're pros," Rae points out. "They surf hard. But that doesn't mean they were trying to outdo you."

"Oh, yeah?" Cricket cries, the words spilling out a mile a minute. "The girls and I were taking turns on the waves, making sure we all got a chance to show Blaine what we could do. But not Shane and his buddies. They were jockeying for position, trying to grab all the best waves."

"That was just for starters," Kanani says, her eyes flashing. "Then they started dropping in on us. I couldn't believe it. They were totally snaking our waves!"

Rae cringes. She's always thought that taking off in front of another surfer and stealing his ride was just about the worst thing you could do. And now her friends are telling her that Shane did that to them.

"Finally," Luna says, "I paddled over to Shane and told him if he dropped in on me one more time I was going to grab his leash and jerk him right off his board. That did it. He and his buddies backed off—at least a little."

Rae's mind is reeling. It's bad enough her mother doesn't like Shane, but why do her friends have to dis him, too? He's a great guy, she *knows* he is. If he wasn't, he wouldn't have agreed to coach her, or invited her to go surfing with him and his famous friends, or promised to introduce her to his sponsors. Besides, no other boy has ever kissed Rae the way Shane did, so passionately she thought her fillings would melt. Only someone with a good heart could do that, right?

"I guess Shane got a little too revved up," she concedes. "He's used to surfing on the pro tour. They go all out in those contests."

"They don't cheat," Isobel declares. She puts her hands on her hips. "That's what snaking waves is— cheating. You know it, Rae, and so do we."

Rae can't believe her ears. "Are you calling my boyfriend a cheater?" she asks angrily.

"If the wet suit fits, wear it," Luna says, and they all laugh.

Rae can feel her ears getting hot. How could Luna— her best friend—be so cruel? *Unless,* Rae thinks, *she isn't a friend at all.*

"You're just jealous," she says, turning to look Luna in the eye. "Up until now, you've been the one with all the advantages—free surfboards, a mother who can coach you, parents who actually want you to be the best surfer you can be. But now I've got something even better—a pro-surfer boyfriend who wants to help me make it onto the tour—and you can't stand it, can you?"

"What are you talking about?" Luna asks incredulously.

"That is so whack," Cricket says, shaking her head.

"Yeah," Isobel agrees, "as if Luna needs someone like Shane to help her get onto the tour."

Kanani looks worried. "What's gotten into you, Rae? Ever since you started hanging with Shane Fox, you're like a different person."

Rae feels trapped. Why are they all ganging up on her? "I'm not the one who's changed!" she cries. "It's you. I mean, I used to think you guys were my friends, but I just don't know anymore."

"Rae! Rae, get over here!"

She looks over at the parking lot. Mom is standing beside the truck, waving her over.

"I gotta go," Rae says miserably. She turns and starts walking back to the parking lot. She can feel the girls' eyes on her, and she imagines she can hear their disapproving whispers.

What else could go wrong? she wonders. She feels torn up inside, abandoned, and totally alone.

And then she remembers her father. *He* still wants her. In fact, he's been phoning her every night, urging her to move to Chicago with him.

When she gets home, she decides, she's going to call him.

12

Yes, of course we could arrange for you to take windsurfing lessons in Chicago," Rae's father says.

Rae grips the receiver tightly. What is she getting herself into? "And . . . and could I buy a windsurfer?"

Dad hesitates. "Well, maybe not right away. Money's a little tight right now, and Chicago is an expensive city. Plus, I'm not sure about the public schools. We might decide you'd be happier in a private school, and that costs a bundle."

"When would I move there?"

"I'm leaving tomorrow to start looking for an apartment. Then I'll have my things shipped out. So actually, you can come pretty much anytime you want. I'm sure you'll want to be there to start school in September."

A new school. That means making new friends. Sounds scary, Rae decides.

But I've alienated all my friends here with my temper this afternoon, she reminds herself. *So what's the difference?*

"Have you talked to Mom about this?" Rae asks anxiously.

"I've brought it up," he replies. "Naturally, she's not delighted with the idea. But it's your choice. Sherri's, too. By the way, have you talked to your sister? What's she thinking?"

"I . . . I don't know. I just started thinking about it myself. I mean," she adds, suddenly panicked at the thought of making a commitment she can't get out of, "I haven't totally decided yet, Dad."

"I understand, Rae Ann. There have been a lot of difficult changes lately, haven't there?"

You don't know the half of it, Dad, Rae thinks.

Dad sighs. "All I can say is this: I love you girls, and I'd love to have you with me full time."

"I love you, too, Dad," Rae says. It's the one thing she can say without hesitation.

"I'll call you from Chicago. Good-bye, my Ray of Sunshine," he adds, using his pet name for her.

Rae feels a tug at her heart. She doesn't want her father to move away. But does she have the guts to go with him? She hangs up and sits there, gnawing the inside of her cheek and wondering.

The sound of the bedroom door opening makes her turn. Sherri is standing there, looking as worried as Rae feels. "Are you going to do it?" she asks.

"Were you eavesdropping?" Rae asks irritably, but deep down, she's almost relieved. Now she doesn't have to think of a way to bring up the subject.

Sherri smiles guiltily and shrugs. "Well, are you?" she asks.

"Moving to Chicago with Dad? I don't know."

"How can you even think of leaving Crescent Cove?" Sherri asks, plopping herself on the bed. "All our friends are here."

Maybe yours are, Rae thinks, but she doesn't say it. She doesn't want to have to explain the whole mess to her sister. "So is Monster Mom," she says instead.

Sherri giggles. "She has been kind of mean lately."

"Kind of?" Rae cries. "She's over the top. And as usual, she's taking it out on me."

"It's not just Mom. You do everything you can to make her mad, too."

"That's not true," Rae snaps. "It's always been easier for you because you've gone along with the horseback-riding stuff. I want to surf. So in her bizarro view of the world, I'm some kind of slacker."

Sherri looks hurt. "You make it sound like I ride horses just to get on Mom's good side. I actually like it, you know."

"I know, I know. But you can do that in Chicago."

"Rae, I don't want to move," Sherri whines. "And I don't want you to go, either." She pauses, looking like she's about to cry. Then she blurts out, "I'd be really sad without you."

Rae can feel her own eyes misting up. "Me, too, shrimp," she whispers.

It's a week later, and Rae is alone in her room, strumming her guitar. "Driving by the beach with the surf so out of reach," she sings mournfully. "Should I stay, should I go? Ooh, I don't know."

That about sums it up, she decides.

For one entire, agonizing week, she's had to spend every morning leading beach rides with her mother. Meanwhile, just a stone's throw away, surfers are shredding the perfect waves of Luna Bay. She watches their takeoffs and cutbacks with a longing that is almost too much to bear. If only she was out there with them!

Almost worse is watching her friends—oops, *ex*-friends—working at surf camp. It makes her heart ache to see them laughing and talking together. She'd give anything to be there with them. Not that she's about to make up or anything. Still, she wouldn't mind giving them a chance to make up with her.

And then there's Shane. He hasn't called, and she can feel their relationship slipping away. Sometimes, as she trots along the water's edge with her mother and another bunch of eager tourists, she sees him surfing the pier, his distinctive yellow and black wet suit gleaming in the sun. *Is he seeing another girl?* she wonders. She's thought of calling him, but she's scared to find out.

Pushing Shane out of her mind, Rae thinks about Dad's latest phone call. He's settling in, living in an apartment his company helped him find. It's only a half a mile from the lake, he says. He jogs there every morning, watching the windsurfers fly across the whitecaps, catching air.

She sighs and sings, "Chicago's like a dream, could I make it in that scene? Should I stay, should I go? Ooh, I don't know."

Rae hugs her guitar to her chest. Lately, singing and writing songs has become her only solace. She wishes she had the guts to perform at the Java Jones Open Mike Night. But Shane's words still ring in her ears: "Maybe you should wait awhile, keep practicing. I'll let you know when you're ready." Only how can he tell her if they never talk?

Besides, didn't Shane say she should concentrate on her number one talent, her surfing? And she wants to—if only she could get away from her uptight, controlling mother. She closes her eyes and pictures herself roaring into a grinding barrel. The heavy lip curls over her head. Is she going to make it? Yes, yes, yes!

Rae opens her eyes and finds herself back in the dreary reality of her room. She feels so frustrated, she could scream. Tossing her guitar on the bed, she jumps to her feet. She should probably start the laundry her mother left for her. But Mom won't be back for at least an hour, so Rae wanders through the house, looking for something that will take her mind off her troubles.

She finds it in the living room. Mom has been working nonstop on the upcoming Day at the Ranch, and the coffee table is strewn with papers, news clippings, and photos of last year's event. Rae sits down and looks through the photographs. The kids look so excited! Some of them had never even patted a horse before, let alone ridden on one. But thanks to Mom and the other volunteers, they'd gotten a chance to forget their troubles and play cowboy for a day.

Rae has to admit that she really admires her mother for thinking up an event like that and pulling it off. Mom has brought all the local trail riders together to do something worthwhile, something important. Rae picks up a news clipping with the headline CRESCENT COVE TRAIL RIDERS SHOW THEY CARE.

Then, suddenly, an inkling of an idea wiggles its way into Rae's consciousness. Wouldn't it be cool to organize a beach day for kids with cancer? She pictures the kids splashing in the waves, building sand castles, exploring tide pools. But that's not all they could do. If some local surfers agreed to help out, the kids could even experience the thrill of surfing! It wouldn't be hard to do. The surfers would simply paddle the kids into the lineup on tandem boards, then catch waves and help the kids stand up.

Rae is so excited, she can barely sit still. She'd love to put together an event like that! And then another thought hits her. Not only would a "Day at the Beach" be fun for the kids, it might also persuade her mother that surfers aren't selfish slackers. Especially if she could find some famous, successful, well-educated surfer to get involved—a surfer her mother would have to agree is a good role model.

Rae racks her brain, trying to come up with the perfect candidate. She runs into her room and leafs through some back issues of *SG Magazine*.

"Bonnie Gormley!" she says out loud, gazing at a photo sequence of a surfer pulling off a jaw-dropping aerial one-eighty. Gormley is a top pro who waited until she finished college before joining the tour. Plus, she's a successful businesswoman who runs her own website about surfing.

Rae runs into her room and turns on her computer, all set to send Bonnie Gormley an E-mail. Then she hesitates. Can she really pull off a huge event like this? She'll have to find sponsors, recruit volunteers, contact hospitals, send out press releases—all the things her mother spends hours and hours doing every year.

Well, why not? she asks herself. It's not impossible. Anyway, it wouldn't hurt to try, especially if it helps to change Mom's mind about surfing.

Rae whips off an e-mail to Bonnie Gormley's website, then sits back and tries to decide which local surfers she should ask to help her organize the event. Of course, the first names that pop into her head are Luna, Kanani, Isobel, and Cricket. But she can't ask them—not after their fight. Well, who then?

The answer is so obvious she can't imagine why she didn't think of it right away. She feels a grin creeping up her cheeks. She's going to ask Shane.

13

"Oh, heavens," Mom says, groaning and looking around the tack shed, "we're out of fly spray."

Rae looks up from the saddle she's polishing. "Do you want me to go to the feed store and buy some?" she asks hopefully.

"Would you? I wouldn't ask, but you know how bad the flies are in this hot weather. And I have about a million phone calls to make this afternoon."

Rae jumps to her feet. She's been waiting for this moment since yesterday morning. "No problem. And can I stop by the mall on the way back?"

"Well . . ."

"Come on, Mom. I've been working my butt off cleaning these saddles. I deserve a break."

Mom smiles and ruffles her hair. "Be back by dinnertime, okay?"

Rae jumps in the car and starts down the driveway. As soon as she's out of earshot, she lets out a whoop of joy. "Now if I can just find Shane," she says, "everything will be perfect!"

She drives to the feed store and buys the fly spray at warp speed, then heads to Crescent Cove Beach Park. There's no sign of Shane, but she runs into some locals who tell her that he was planning to surf Paintball Point this afternoon. Five minutes later, she's at the Point, jogging down the trail that leads from the parking lot to the beach. And there he is, sitting out in the lineup.

Rae's heart leaps into her throat. She waves to Shane, and eventually he spots her. He grabs a wave and rides in.

Her heart is pounding as he walks toward her. It's been over a week since they've talked, but she's thought about him constantly. And now here he is, looking totally hot, with sand on his eyebrows and droplets of water spraying from his spiky blond hair.

"So you finally broke out of that prison, huh?" he says, flashing his killer smile.

"Kind of," she replies. "At least for a couple of hours." She shrugs. "Hey, I heard you made it to the surf session at Carson Beach last weekend."

He frowns. "What's with those girlfriends of yours? They were totally tweaked, just because Blaine wanted to photograph me and my crew. I mean, we're the pros, right? Why wouldn't he want to shoot us?"

"But the girls said you were snaking their waves."

Shane laughs disdainfully. "We didn't take a number and wait in line, if that's what you mean. But those girls aren't exactly shy and reserved, either. We were surfing hard—all of us." He shakes his head. "I don't know what their problem is."

"It was my fault, really," Rae says apologetically. "Blaine asked Cricket if he could photograph our crew—just the five of us girls. I wasn't really supposed to invite you."

"Yeah? Well, I notice that didn't stop Blaine from photographing me." He smiles a cocky smile. "I guess he must have seen something he liked."

Rae looks away. Shane could at least be a little bit understanding, she thinks. After all, it was the girls' photo session, their very first one. Shane, on the other hand, has had his photo in a couple of surf magazines already.

In that instant, Rae gets a glimpse of Shane as her girlfriends see him—as *she* used to see him—and she doesn't like it. But before she can figure out what that means exactly, a tall surfer with nut-brown skin and shoulder-length salt-and-pepper hair steps up behind Shane.

"It takes a lot to get Shane Fox out of the water," he

declares. "I figured I'd better come in and meet the girl who can do it."

"This is my friend, Rae," Shane says. "Rae, this is Goose Takaya, the president of Edge Surfwear."

Rae can feel her jaw dropping. Goose Takaya isn't just the president of Edge. He's also a legendary Hawaiian surfer, a top pro back in the eighties. She snaps her mouth shut and manages a stammering, "Hi."

"Rae is a pretty happening amateur," Shane says. "She came in second in the Western Championship."

Goose is looking at her with interest, and instantly, Rae forgets she was ever upset with Shane. "Thanks," she says, blushing scarlet.

"I'd like to see you surf sometime," Goose says. "Do you have your board with you?"

"No," she answers. "I—I didn't know—"

"You can use mine," Shane breaks in.

Rae hesitates. Can she impress Goose on a borrowed board? Besides, she doesn't have a wet suit, or even a bathing suit.

"Come on," Goose says. "Catch a few." He shoots her an encouraging smile. "If you're game."

Rae knows she may never have this chance again. She'd be a fool to say no. "Okay."

She throws off her flip-flops, takes Shane's surfboard, and paddles out in her shorts and T-shirt. Out in the lineup, she sits on the board and tries to calm down. Talk about pressure! Goose and Shane are standing on the sand, watching her intently. Borrowed board or not, she's got to show them what she can do.

She waits for a set, then waits even longer as two other surfers take the first and second waves. The set wave is a solid four-foot grinder. She takes off, bottom-turns hard, and cruises for a second or two, feeling out the new board. Then she hits the lip and snaps back just as the wave starts to pitch out. She flies into the tube, comes out the other side, and pulls off two more cutbacks before the wave closes out.

Rae's heart is sailing as she paddles back out. "Pay attention, Goose," she says under her breath. "Rae Perrault is on the way up!"

She catches two more decent waves, then paddles back in. As she jogs out of the water, T-shirt dripping, Shane and Goose are smiling at her.

"Sweet," Goose says simply.

Shane nods. Rae giggles foolishly. She can't help it. She's just so happy!

"So, what's your next move?" Goose asks. "Are you competing in Edge's Rude Girl Open at San Onofre next month?"

How can Rae tell Goose the truth—that she won't be competing at all if her mother has her way? She can't. So instead she says, "Right now I'm kind of busy. I'm trying to set up a charity event. I'm calling it 'A Day at the Beach.' It's for kids with cancer. I want to bring them to the beach and show them how to surf."

"Kids with cancer?" Shane repeats dubiously. "Aren't those kids way too sick to surf?"

"A lot of them aren't. My mother runs a similar event called a Day at the Ranch. The kids get to ride horses, play games, have a picnic. They love it."

"Tell me more," Goose says.

"Well, I'm hoping to find a bunch of surfers who will volunteer to take the kids out on tandem boards. There will be other events, too—like building sand castles and face painting."

"It sounds like a lot of work," Shane declares. "Do you really think you can pull it off?"

Rae hesitates. She's been wondering that herself. But Goose says matter-of-factly, "The first thing you need is a major sponsor. Someone who will lend you wet suits and softboards. And helmets—you'll want the kids protected. And you'll need bags of goodies to give away. Sunblock, lip gloss, that sort of thing."

"That would be perfect!" Rae agrees eagerly.

"You call my office first thing tomorrow morning," Goose says. "Shane will give you the number. I think Edge would be willing to get behind an event like this."

Rae can feel her eyes bugging out. "Really? That would be incredible!"

"You can count me in," Shane says. "Having a pro on board will be good publicity. Plus I can sign autographs for the kids."

"I'm going to ask our entire team to volunteer," Goose replies. He glances at Shane. "Ready to head back out?"

"I'll meet you out there. I want to walk Rae back to her car."

"Call me tomorrow, Rae," Goose calls over his shoulder. "I'm stoked!"

As soon as Goose is in the water, Rae throws her arms around Shane. "Thank you, thank you, thank you!" she cries.

"For what?" He chuckles, hugging her back.

"For talking me up to Goose Takaya. For lending me your board. For saying you'd help with A Day at the Beach. You're the best!"

"You're pretty fine yourself," he replies. "Goose really went for your idea. I think we both scored some points."

Is that all Shane cares about? Rae wonders. *Scoring points?* Then she reminds herself that she's hoping to score some points, too. She's trying to convince Mom to let her start surfing again.

Still, that's not her only reason for wanting to put on A Day at the Beach. She remembers the happy smiles on the faces of the kids who attended A Day at the Ranch last year. *They'll be even happier when they get a chance to go surfing,* she thinks with satisfaction.

Her thoughts are cut short when Shane leans down to kiss her. Right now she's scoring points with Shane, and that's all that matters.

14

"So what's this?" Rae asks, pointing to a page of names, addresses, and phone numbers. "The list of volunteers?"

Mom is sitting at the kitchen table, piles of papers stacked in front of her. Each one relates to some aspect of A Day at the Ranch. Rae is by her side, soaking up information the way she slurps up a smoothie.

"That's right," Mom replies, sipping her coffee. "See how I've put a letter beside each name—either an *H, F, G,* or *M*? That tells me if the person can supervise a horseback ride, serve food, or run a game. The *M* stands for Miscellaneous. Those people stuff goody bags, do cleanup, that sort of thing."

"Okay, what next?" Rae asks, rubbing her hands.

"Well, I've already sent each volunteer a letter, telling them the date and time of the event. Now I have to call each person and remind them one more time, see if they have any questions. That's an important step. People say they're going to volunteer, but then the day comes and they completely forget."

Rae shakes her head in awe. Mom really has this organization thing down cold. If only she could enlist her mother to help her run A Day at the Beach! But that's not possible, so she'll just have to keep her ears open and learn as much as she can.

Sherri walks through the room, lugging a basket of laundry. "How come Rae doesn't have to do laundry?" she grumbles.

"Because she's helping me with A Day at the Ranch," Mom replies.

"I can help, too," Sherri insists.

"You can help later when we start stuffing envelopes. Right now Rae and I need to work on this press release." When Sherri doesn't move, she adds, "Aileen is picking you up in less than an hour, right? If you still want to go to the movies, get cracking!"

Sherri shoots Rae a dirty look and leaves. Rae can't believe it. For once *she's* the good girl, the one Mom wants around. It sure feels nice for a change. And what's more, she doesn't have to fake it. She really does want to help Mom plan A Day at the Ranch.

Mom gets up to refill her coffee. "We've been working hard all morning."

"Every morning all week," Rae adds.

Mom nods. "So why don't we take a break this afternoon and go for a horseback ride?"

"Well . . ."

"I know, I know. It's not your favorite activity." She shrugs, looking a little sad. "I just thought maybe we could ride up to Cabrillo Ridge. There's a nest of baby owls in one of the juniper trees."

Rae considers. It might be kind of nice to go for a ride without a bunch of tourists along for a change. Besides, she can tell her mother really wants her to say yes.

"Why not?" Rae replies.

Mom beams. "Okay, let me just get this press release sent off. Then we'll have some lunch and head out."

An hour later, Rae and Mom are cantering their horses up Cabrillo Ridge. It's a beautiful day for a ride, cool and clear, and the horses are full of energy. The wind blows Rae's hair as she urges Moose on. Just like Moose, she's happy to be moving.

At the top of the ridge, they slow the horses to a walk. Mom's face is flushed and her eyes are shining.

"Look at that view!" she exclaims. The landscape stretches out below them—rolling hills dotted with oak trees, and beyond that, the town of Crescent Cove and the sea. "I love it here!"

Mom looks happy to be alive, and Rae realizes it's been a long time since she's seen her mother like that. All those months of fighting with Dad, and then the breakup, must have really worn her down.

And I guess I didn't help much, Rae admits to herself. She feels guilty just thinking about it.

"The owls are over here," Mom says, leading the way to a stand of juniper trees. "Look," she whispers, pointing to an upper branch where a mother owl is keeping watch. The owl spots Rae and her mother and hoots a warning.

"She's enormous!" Rae exclaims.

"And there are the babies."

From a nest perched close to the tree trunk, four baby owls peer out at them.

"They're so sweet!" Rae cries.

Suddenly a second adult owl glides over their heads and lands in a nearby tree. In his mouth is a dead mouse.

"That must be the father," Rae says. She giggles. "He brought takeout."

The father owl delivers the dead mouse to the nest, where the babies eagerly pick it apart. Then he joins the mother on the juniper branch. They peer intently at Rae and Mom with an expression that seems to say, "Stay away from our babies!"

"Come on," Mom whispers. "We've disturbed them long enough." She continues down the trail with Rae following. At a bend in the trail, they reach an open meadow. "Let's stop for a snack," Mom suggests.

They tie up the horses and find a flat, wide rock to

sit on. Mom opens the saddlebags and takes out apples and bottled water. As they eat, she gazes across the meadow and sighs. "It's a lot of work raising children. I'm just glad I don't have four of them."

Rae sips her water. "I guess two is bad enough," she ventures.

Mom looks at her, then smiles. "Don't get me wrong. I love being a mother. I just didn't realize it was going to be so challenging." She pauses thoughtfully. "My mother had it easier, I think. There was just me, and I was the kind of girl who was eager to please. My mother was a horsewoman, so I rode horses. It was expected of me, and it made my mother happy. That's all I needed to know."

"It's not that I don't like horseback riding," Rae says. "Honest, Mom. It's just that I *love* surfing."

"I know, hon. And if it was just a hobby, I'd say fine. But when you talk about making surfing your career, I have to put my foot down."

"But why?"

"It's the whole atmosphere that troubles me. Surfers are obsessed with surfing. I want you to have a broader life experience—to be well educated and cultured. What kind of life would you have, traveling around the world with people who only know two things—surfing and partying?"

"Mom, not all surfers are beach bums," Rae insists,

leaning forward to make her point. "The professionals are top athletes. They can't afford to mess up their bodies."

"Well, what about that Shane boy? Dropping out of school to compete! And what an attitude that kid has—he practically gallops my horse into a wall and all he can think to say is, 'That was trippy!' "

Rae snickers, but deep down, she has to agree her mother is right. It wouldn't have hurt Shane to say he was sorry. "I think he was kind of stunned," she suggests. "Anyway, he would apologize if he ever had a chance to come back." She doesn't know if it's true, but she wants to believe it.

Mom looks ready to say something caustic. Then she puts her hand over her mouth and takes a deep breath. "Maybe I'm wrong, Rae. I don't know. I'm not sure I'm thinking straight lately. Living alone has been a big adjustment for me. I'm so used to having your father around. Of course, I haven't liked many of his opinions lately, but at least it gave me something to react to. Now I'm on my own. It's hard."

"Maybe you and Dad should get back together," Rae says hopefully.

But Mom shakes her head. "No, I think we made the right decision. We just have to get used to living a new way. And we will. But meanwhile, we may make a few mistakes. I hope you and your sister can understand that."

Rae looks at her mother's worried face and her heart swells with love. "Sure, Mom. But look, if I can prove to you that surfers today are different than you think—if I can show you that they care about a lot of important, worthwhile things—will you let me start surfing again?"

Mom frowns. "Oh, Rae, I don't know."

"Please? At least say you'll consider it."

"Okay," Mom reluctantly agrees, "I'll consider it."

Rae thrusts her fist in the air and gazes toward the heavens. "Yes!" she cries. "Yes!"

"And you could promise enough ribs to feed fifty children and twenty volunteers?" Rae says into the phone.

"We're always happy to help local charities," answers the manager of the local Food Mart. "You put your request in writing and I'll make sure it happens."

"Oh, thank you!" Rae exclaims. "I'll send the letter today!"

Rae hangs up the phone and does an impromptu victory dance around the room. Ever since her horse-back ride with her mother yesterday, she's been totally pumped. She's going to pull this event off—she has to! Not just for the kids, but for herself.

She glances at the clock. Mom will be home soon. Just enough time for a couple more calls. She reaches for the phone just as it starts to ring.

"Hello?"

"Rae, it's Isobel."

Rae's heart skips a beat. It's been two weeks since she's talked to her friends. In fact, she'd almost resigned herself to the depressing possibility that she would never talk to them again.

"Hi," she says in a shaky voice.

"Rae, Barrels is in trouble."

"What?" Rae gasps. "What kind of trouble?"

"He's been a problem at everyone's house—everything from chasing cats to eating food off the counter to chewing through Cricket's fence," Isobel explains. "Our parents won't let any of us keep him anymore."

"But then where is he?" Rae asks.

"At the animal shelter."

"The shelter! No!"

"Our parents talked to each other on the phone and decided. They said Barrels needs a home with someone who has the time and patience to teach him some manners."

"But Barrels belongs to us!" Rae cries. "Besides, what if no one adopts him?"

"That's just it. If he isn't adopted in thirty days, there's a good chance he'll be put to sleep. That's why we've come up with a plan."

"All right," Rae says. "What is it?"

"Luna went to the library and took out some dog-training books. We're going to visit Barrels at the shelter every day and work with him. We figure maybe if he learns to obey, our parents will let us take him back."

"Good idea. Listen, I'll come with you tomorrow. I've watched my mother train our dogs and I know a little bit about—"

"Rae," Isobel says quietly, "I don't think that's a good idea."

Rae frowns. "Why not?"

There's a long pause. Then she says, "The girls don't know I'm calling you. I'm not sure they want to see you."

"Oh," Rae says, her heart sinking into her knees. She hardens her voice and asks, "Then why did *you* call?"

"I don't know. I just . . . well, you love Barrels just as much as the rest of us. It didn't seem fair not to tell you what's going on."

Rae tries to ignore the painful throbbing in her chest. "Thanks, Isobel," she says flatly.

"I—I just thought you'd want to know," Isobel repeats. Then the phone goes dead.

15

"Right this way," the animal shelter volunteer says, escorting Rae down a narrow hallway. "Let me know if there's one special dog that strikes your fancy."

The volunteer opens a door and Rae walks into a room full of dog runs. Some of the dogs jump to their feet when they see her, barking and wagging their tails. Others merely open an eye or lift an ear. A few huddle in the back corners of their runs, fearful of anything that smells like a human being.

Rae walks down the rows, hoping against hope that Barrels hasn't already been adopted. And then she sees him! He's sleeping on his back with his furry little legs stuck in the air.

"Barrels!" Rae exclaims.

He opens one eye, sniffs, then leaps to his feet and runs to meet her. Rae reaches her hand through the cage and pets him. "Oh, Barrels, you naughty dog! I can't believe you got thrown out of five different houses."

Barrels gazes at her innocently and licks her hand.

"But don't worry," she continues soothingly, "the girls are going to teach you some manners. I'd like to help, but . . ." Her voice trails off and she lets out a sigh.

Rae has thought long and hard about why Isobel called her the other day. Was it just to tell her about Barrels? Or was she trying to reach out to Rae, to rekindle their friendship?

Heaven knows, that's what Rae would like to believe. But what is she supposed to do about it? Call the girls? Show up at their houses, or at the shelter when they come to train Barrels?

And what will happen when the subject of Shane Fox comes up again? Should she defend him? Keep her mouth shut? She just doesn't know.

The shelter volunteer arrives to escort Rae and Barrels into a grassy courtyard. "He needs to stay on the leash," the volunteer tells Rae.

But tell that to Barrels! He runs in circles, knotting the leash and practically tripping Rae. Finally, she gives up and sits in the grass to pet him.

"Why does Shane have to be such an intense guy?" she asks the little dog. "I mean, that's an outstanding trait when you're in a surf contest, but the rest of the time it just seems to offend people."

Barrels looks at her questioningly.

"Okay, so maybe sometimes he offends me, too," she admits. "But what am I supposed to do about it? If I call him on it, he'll get mad. I can't risk that, not if it means losing him and everything he's offering me. I mean, Barrels, Shane is a pro. He knows all the surfers on the tour, all the sponsors, all the inside info. Besides, he's hot!"

Rae feels eyes watching her. An elderly couple with a miniature schnauzer are staring at her, obviously wondering why she's having a long, one-sided conversation with a dog. Blushing, Rae clears her throat and stands up. "Come on, Barrels," she says, "time to go back."

But Barrels will have none of it. He takes off across the courtyard, sideswiping the schnauzer and almost knocking down the couple. It takes Rae and the shelter volunteer five minutes to finally catch him and force him back into his cage.

Rae shakes her head and thinks, *The girls have their work cut out for them.*

Rae checks her E-mail for the tenth time that day. Still no message from Bonnie Gormley. And it's been two whole weeks since Rae wrote to her.

She's probably on a surf trip to Tahiti or some other

exotic place, Rae decides. She's not the type to ignore her fans.

Rae tries not to be disappointed—inviting Bonnie was a real long shot, anyway—but it's hard. There's not another pro surfer in the world who would impress Rae's mom as much as Bonnie Gormley. The woman's got brains, talent, *and* a social conscience.

"Get over it, Rae," she tells herself. Then she plops down on her bed and turns her attention to her Master Checklist, a list of all the things that need to be done to pull off A Day at the Beach. The checklist is something she created after watching her mother make one for A Day at the Ranch, and so far, it's been a godsend.

First, Rae goes over the things that are already accomplished. "Call Edge to confirm delivery of softboards, wet suits, helmets, and goody bags—check," she reads. "Call Food Mart to confirm delivery of food— check. Call city to reserve barbecue pits—check. Call hospitals to publicize event (while making sure the staff promises not to tell Mom)—check."

Rae smiles. Mom may still find out, but how great would it be to take her to the beach on the day of the event and surprise her? She crosses her fingers and continues down the list.

To her amazement, there's only one thing left: line up volunteers. And that means contacting Shane. Not a bad job, in Rae's opinion.

She checks her watch. Mom won't be home from her Trail Riding Club meeting for at least two hours. Quickly, Rae changes her clothes, bends at the waist to fluff up her mussed red hair, and hops in the car to look for Shane.

He's not at the pier and no one has seen him, so she heads over to Crescent Cove Beach Park. Nope. She's about to leave when she spots Shane heading up Surf Street toward Smooth Moves. The sight of him in his bathing suit and a muscle shirt makes her heart zing around her chest like a Ping-Pong ball.

"Shane!" she calls, trotting after him. "Wait up!"

He turns and breaks into his toothy shark smile. "Hey, Red," he says. "Howzit?"

Red! He's got a nickname for her. She giggles like a toddler. "I'm okay. I've been really busy planning the Day at the Beach event."

"Oh, yeah," he says. "Goose told me you're going through with that. When is it, anyway?"

"The first of next month. And, Shane, that's what I want to talk to you about. I—"

"Hang on," he says. "I've been surfing all afternoon and I'm beat. Let's get a smoothie and sit down."

They both order a Peanut Butter Fudge Fury. *Just like the first time we met,* she thinks dreamily.

They grab their smoothies and find a table on the front patio. "I haven't seen you in the water for weeks," he says, slurping his drink. "Why don't we drive down the coast this weekend and see what's breaking?"

"I can't, Shane," she says sadly. "My mother won't let me surf, remember?"

"And you're still sticking around? When are you going to learn you don't have to do what she tells you? If Mommy Dearest won't let you follow your dream, it's time to say bye-bye, Mommy."

"That's why I'm planning the Day at the Beach," she explains. "Well, partly, anyway. My mother said if I could prove to her that modern surfers are interested in more than just surfing and partying, she'd consider letting me surf again."

"Sounds like a lot of work to convince her of something you could be doing anyway," he declares.

Rae isn't sure what to say. Does he want her to move out? She's thought of it a few times, that's for sure. But where would she go—except Chicago, that is? And how would she survive? It's all too overwhelming to think about.

"Anyway, Shane," she says, shoving her confusing thoughts aside, "it's time to start signing up volunteers. Will you put the word out to all your friends, and to the Edge surf team?"

"When did you say this beach thing was?" he asks, stretching out his legs.

"The first, from one to four."

He frowns. "Uh-uh. That's the day of the Ventura County Classic. I'm supposed to compete."

Rae can feel her shoulders drooping. "But Shane, you told me you'd help."

"Look, Rae," Shane replies, "helping sick kids is nice, for sure. But I can do that some other time. My career comes first."

"But the Ventura Classic isn't even a pro event! Can't you just get out of it?" Before he can answer, she reaches out and takes his hand. "Please, Shane. I've spent so many hours organizing this, and I was counting on you to round up some strong, confident surfers who can get the kids up safely."

Shane slips his hand away and pats hers gently. "Rae, baby, I don't want you to be disappointed, but I gotta tell you the truth. Even if it wasn't the same weekend as the Ventura Classic, not many pro surfers are going to want to volunteer their time on a charity event like this. If you were raising money for Surfrider Foundation, okay. But let's face it—kids with cancer are a downer. I just get into stuff with a more positive vibe. Sun, sand, surf, smoothies. All the S words," he adds with a laugh.

Rae looks away, too confused and troubled to speak. Is Shane right? Will surfers pass on A Day at the Beach because it's a downer? But Mom's Day at the Ranch wasn't that way at all. The kids were laughing and running around, and the volunteers had the time of their lives.

Besides, Rae can't believe all surfers will be turned off. Goose Takaya was stoked, wasn't he? He even agreed to sponsor the event, and that was a major commitment.

Rae looks at Shane, leaning back in his chair, sipping his smoothie with a self-satisfied smile on his face. *He doesn't care one bit that he's letting me down,* she realizes with dismay. *Not one bit.*

And in that moment, the mask falls away, and Rae sees Shane the way her girlfriends see him. The way *she* used to see him before she let herself get hypnotized by his big talk and promises.

And what have his promises actually done for me? she wonders.

Oh, sure, she's gotten a few surfing tips and met a few famous surfers—people she probably could have met on her own. On the other hand, she's caused trouble for her mother, alienated her friends, and allowed Shane to convince her she can't do much of anything without his approval.

But no longer. She gets to her feet and says, "Yeah, you're into the S words, Shane, that's for sure. Selfish, spoiled, and stupid."

Shane looks around the patio anxiously. "Sit down, Rae," he hisses. "Everybody's staring at you."

"Oh, I'm sorry, Shane, I forgot. They're only allowed to stare at you, right? Well, I'll give them something to stare at." She picks up her smoothie and points at Shane. "Here he is, folks," she says loudly. "The famous pro surfer, Shane Fox! Take a good look."

Then she pulls the lid off her smoothie and pours her Peanut Butter Fudge Fury on his head.

Are you back to see the little black-and-brown dog?" asks the animal shelter volunteer, leading Rae down the hallway.

"Yes. How is he?"

"Fine. But I think you should know that a group of four girls has been coming to see him every day. I suspect they'll be adopting him soon."

"Thanks for telling me."

Does that mean Barrels has learned to obey? she wonders.

The volunteer gives Rae a leash and opens the cage. Barrels scampers out and jumps into Rae's arms, barking eagerly. She sets him down and says, "Heel." To her amazement, Barrels runs to her left side and looks up at her expectantly. She walks toward the courtyard and he walks beside her, looking like a photo in an obedience-training book.

"Wow!" Rae breathes.

But all that ends when they reach the courtyard. Barrels takes off, running in circles like a prisoner who's just been released from solitary confinement.

"Barrels, stop!" Rae calls. "Come here!"

He ignores her and begins digging a hole in the flowerbed. Rae rushes over and snaps the leash on his collar before he knows what hit him. She lowers herself onto the grass and pulls him into her lap. "Chill, boy. Our parents aren't going to let you come home if you keep acting like that."

Barrels responds by rolling onto his back and presenting his belly for her to scratch. She laughs and says, "Barrels, you are impossible!"

She's trying to find the spot that makes his leg involuntarily jump when she notices the door to the courtyard opening. She looks up, and her heart kicks into overdrive. It's the girls!

They spot her an instant later. She can see them hesitate, glance at each other, then walk slowly toward her. The look on their faces is a mix of confusion, self-consciousness, and uncertainty.

Barrels's emotions are a lot more straightforward. He jumps up and runs toward them, barking and wagging his tail. Then he runs back to Rae. Then back to them again.

"Hi," Rae says, getting to her feet.

"How did you know we'd be here?" Luna asks.

"I didn't, but—" She glances anxiously at Isobel. "I—I did know you were training Barrels."

"I told her," Isobel admits. "I thought she had a right to know what was happening."

Luna nods. "I've been meaning to call you, Rae. I just . . . I didn't know what to say, or if you even wanted to talk to me."

"I've wanted to call you, too," Cricket admits. "I don't want to fight, Rae."

Kanani nods. "You're one of my very best friends. I feel really bad about what happened."

"You?" Rae cries. "I'm the one who invited Shane to your surf session. That was totally out of line. And the way Shane snaked your waves was out of line, too— but not exactly out of character."

Luna looks puzzled. "I didn't think you saw it that way."

"I didn't," Rae admits. "But since our fight, I learned a lot more about Shane Fox." She puts her hands on her hips. "He's a controlling, arrogant, self-centered brat."

Cricket giggles. "That's what we were trying to tell you!"

"Yeah, but I wasn't ready to hear it," Rae says. "I'm really sorry. I was too starstruck to see anything but what I wanted to see."

"So what happened between you two?" Luna asks. "I mean, what changed your mind?"

"He totally bailed on my Day at the Beach" she complains. "And after he promised he'd help me round up volunteers!"

"Day at the Beach? Volunteers? What are you talking about?" Isobel asks with a bewildered frown.

And suddenly Rae realizes how much she has to tell the girls. They sit in a circle in the grass, and while Barrels moves from girl to girl, begging for attention, she explains all about her idea to put on A Day at the Beach.

"So not only will we be helping kids with cancer experience the thrill of surfing," Rae concludes, "I'll also be convincing my mother that surfers are caring, compassionate people."

"Brilliant!" Luna exclaims.

"Totally!" Isobel agrees.

"What do you need us to do?" Kanani asks.

Rae grins at her friends. It feels so good to be with them again, sharing her feelings and getting their support. "Well, I want you to volunteer, of course," she says. "And I need you to help me round up other surfers who will agree to get involved."

"Hey, I know!" exclaims Cricket, producing a bag of M&Ms from her pocket and passing them around. "I'll call Blaine Barker. He's always traveling up and down the coast, photographing the best surfers on the best days. I'll ask him to spread the word."

"Perfect!" Rae says. "And ask him if he knows Bonnie Gormley. I sent her an E-mail asking her to come, but she never wrote back. She's like the ultimate surfing role model, and I want my mom to meet her."

"I want to meet her, too," Kanani says.

"But wait," Luna breaks in, "are you telling me Shane wouldn't volunteer?"

"He said he would," Rae explains, "but then he found out the Ventura County Classic is on the same day. He said his career is more important than helping a bunch of downer cancer patients."

The girls gasp. "You want we should off him, boss?" Isobel asks with a smirk.

"I already took care of it. I dumped my smoothie on his head!"

Five minutes later, when the girls have finally stopped laughing, Rae says, "We've been out here a long time. The shelter workers are going to think we kidnapped Barrels."

"We're going to do better than that," Luna says. "We're adopting him today!"

Rae is dubious. "You think he's ready?"

"Not really," Luna admits. "But we're not going to take him home—not yet. We're going to hide him somewhere until we can turn him into the perfect dog."

"Hide him?" Rae repeats. "Where?"

"In the surf shop storage room, or the shed behind

my house, or your mom's horse trailer," Isobel says. "We may have to move him around, but we'll manage."

"It's better than letting him stay here and get adopted by someone else," Cricket says. She shudders. "Or worse."

"Okay," Rae says with a determined nod. "Let's go, Barrels." The little dog runs over, and she grabs his leash.

"Ask him to heel," Kanani says.

She looks so eager that Rae can't bring herself to reveal what happened last time. "Heel!" she orders.

Barrels heels and the girls smile with pleasure. They all start walking toward the courtyard door. At the last second, Barrels makes a run for it. The leash flies out of Rae's hand and he's off, veering back and forth across the courtyard like a rabbit with a fox on its tail.

The girls let out a groan and Luna says, "I don't know which is going to be tougher—organizing this charity event or training Barrels."

Rae grins at her. Nothing can dampen her spirits—not with her best friends beside her again. "Together," she says, "we'll pull them both off."

17

"Would you please tell me where we're going?" Mom begs, reaching up to adjust the blindfold that covers her eyes.

In the backseat, Sherri cries, "Don't touch that! She's trying to peek, Rae."

"Relax, Mom," Rae says. "We're almost there."

Mom fidgets in the seat, and Rae stifles a laugh. It's hilarious watching Mom try to handle a situation where she's not in control. It almost makes Rae want to drive around a little longer, just to watch her squirm.

But that would be too mean, Rae decides. Anyway, they have to get to the beach before the kids arrive. Or in Rae's case, *back* to the beach.

Rae met the other girls at Crescent Cove Beach Park at six o'clock that morning. Rae was touched that even

David showed up to help pitch in. They all spent the next two hours setting up for A Day at the Beach. First they put up the tents (borrowed from Shoreline Surf Camp). Then the Edge Surfwear people showed up with the wet suits, softboards, helmets, and goodie bags. After all the equipment was organized and the goodie bags were spread out on a tables, the girls roped off the sand castle–building area (with sand tools donated by the local hardware store). Finally, Rae left the others to clean off the picnic tables while she went to pick up Mom and Sherri.

Now Rae pulls into the beach parking lot. With Sherri's help, she leads Mom to the beach. The rest of the girls, along with Luna's parents, gather round to watch.

"Okay, Mom," Rae says, "you can look now."

Mom takes off the blindfold and blinks at the surf-boards, the wet suits, the tents, and the tables heaped with goodie bags. She sees the girls and Luna's parents grinning at her. Finally, she spots the banner that says WELCOME TO THE FIRST ANNUAL DAY AT THE BEACH.

"Wha-what is all this?" she asks, looking bewildered.

"My answer to your Day at the Ranch," Rae replies. "Except today the kids won't be riding horses. They'll be surfing waves."

Mom's jaw goes slack. She looks around again. "Who organized this?" she asks at last.

"Rae did," Sherri pipes up.

Mom stares at Rae. "But how—? When—? I mean, you couldn't possibly have done this all by yourself!"

"Practically," Luna breaks in. "She organized everything, lined up all the sponsors, called the hospitals. All we did was help out when she asked us to."

"Which wasn't very often," Isobel adds.

Mom gazes at Rae with a combination of amazement, admiration, and awe. It's a look Rae has never seen her mother direct at her before, and it feels good. So good, in fact, that Rae barely knows how to react. She giggles and shrugs stupidly.

But Mom knows exactly what to do. She throws her arms around Rae and hugs her so tight that Rae is certain her ribs will snap. "I am so proud of you!" Mom whispers in her ear. Then she releases Rae and says with gusto, "I'm ready to work. What do you want me to do?"

Before Rae can answer, the first volunteers show up—five local surfers recruited by Luna's parents. Barrels, who was lying in the sand chewing a stick, decides it's his job to be the official greeter. He jumps up and charges, barking wildly.

"Barrels, come here!" Rae calls firmly.

The little dog stops, turns, and trots over to her.

"Sit," Rae says. He sits. "Lie down." He lies down.

"Hang on," Mom says with a puzzled frown. "Isn't

that the dog you brought to the house? The one that scared my horses and ripped up my flowerbeds?"

"The same," Rae says.

"What did you do—give him shock treatments?"

Rae laughs. "We trained him, that's all."

"And hid him in the surf shop storage room for two weeks," Luna's dad breaks in.

"Well, we couldn't let him stay at the shelter!" Luna retorts.

Her dad chuckles. "I couldn't figure out how our new line of beach towels got covered with brown hair. Little did I know Barrels was sleeping on them!"

Rae's mom laughs. "You girls are just full of surprises lately."

"And Luna's parents said we can keep Barrels," Rae says eagerly. "He'll stay at Luna's house and go to surf camp every day. But he'll belong to all of us girls."

That's the last relaxed conversation Rae and her mother manage before things swing into high gear. Soon the rest of the volunteers show up, and Rae takes them aside to thank them and give them a pep talk. Goose Takaya arrives a few minutes later, realizes he knows Luna's parents, and goes over to help them start the barbecues. Then a Food Mart truck coasts into the parking lot and Mom takes over, instructing the driver where to unload the food.

Not long after that, the kids show up, driven to the

beach in buses rented by the hospitals. They are children of every age, shape, color, and size—from a skinny six-year-old girl with skin so pale you can almost see through it, to a strapping seventeen-year-old boy who has lost his hair from chemotherapy.

"They look so normal," Cricket breathes. "Like regular kids."

"They *are* regular kids," Rae replies. "But they've been through a lot. So come on, let's show them a good time."

Soon the beach is crowded with happy, shouting, laughing kids, all wearing rash guards (provided by Shoreline Surf Shop) with the words LIFE IS A DAY AT THE BEACH across the front. Some of them are building sand castles, some are opening their goodie bags, some are sunbathing or throwing Frisbees or kicking Nerf footballs.

Rae rounds up a group of five kids and leads them over to the wet suits. Some volunteers help them find their sizes and get suited up. When they're ready, Rae lines them up in front of a row of surfboards and gives them a beginning surf lesson. Then they pile into kayaks and paddle out to Black Rock.

The rest of the girls are already out there, floating in the lineup on long tandem softboards. Rae and the other kayakers deliver one kid to each girl, and the kids climb onto the boards.

Some of the kids are obviously nervous, but the girls joke around to reassure them.

"Are there sharks out here?" a girl asks.

"If you see one, will you take a photo for me?" Kanani replies. "Tell him to smile."

"I can't even swim," one boy confides.

"If everything goes well, you won't have to," Cricket says.

"What if we wipe out?" another child asks.

Rae looks puzzled. Then she snaps her fingers. "I've got an idea—hold your breath!"

Now everyone is loosening up, giggling and teasing each other. Rae looks over her shoulder. A set is coming in. "Remember," she calls, "when your partner puts her hands on your waist, that's your cue to stand up!"

Luna is the first to take off. She paddles into a perfect three-foot wave while her partner, a girl about ten with rows of slender black braids, kneels in front of her. The wave crests and Luna stands up. She reaches forward and grasps the girl's waist. The little girl gets to her knees, teeters—then, with Luna's help, she's up and riding!

Luna and the girl are flying across the face of the wave. The girl lifts her arms and shrieks with delight. On shore, Blaine Barker snaps photos of each rider.

Rae watches from the kayak, her heart soaring in triumph. The kids look so happy, so excited! "Yes!" she shouts as each child stands up. "Look at you! You're surfing!"

It isn't until lunchtime that Rae thinks about Shane. In the weeks since they broke up, she's seen him around maybe five or six times. Each time, the sight of his pale blue eyes and killer smile sends a pang of longing through her heart. Now, however, she tries to picture him here, serving the barbecued ribs, talking and joking with the kids, building sand castles and throwing Frisbees—but she can't.

He wouldn't be happy at an event like this, she realizes, unless he was the center of attention. He's never happy unless he is.

It's at that moment that Rae knows she's truly over Shane. She glances at the other volunteers as they pass out napkins, clean up trash, and talk to the kids. Any one of them would be more interesting than Shane, she decides. Like that boy over there—the one with the shaggy brown hair, wearing the Sola Beach Lifeguard T-shirt. He's not bad at all!

"Hey, Rae," Luna says suddenly, elbowing her friend, "is that who I think it is?"

Rae looks up and sees a tall blond woman in her thirties walking toward her. She does a double take and gasps. It's Bonnie Gormley!

"Excuse me," the woman says, "is Rae Perrault here?"

"Um . . . that's me," Rae squeaks.

Bonnie shakes her hand. "I'm Bonnie Gormley. I'm sorry I didn't respond to your e-mail. I just got back from Hawaii and I haven't checked my website messages for quite a while."

"But then how—?" Rae begins.

"Kate Martin called my office and left a voice mail." She laughs. "Kate Martin is a very famous name in women's surfing, as I'm sure you know. I called her back immediately and she put your friend Luna on the phone. I was impressed with your idea, and just what lengths your friends were willing to go to for you. I wouldn't miss this event for anything."

"Wow, thanks!" Rae exclaims.

Bonnie has shown up with her own goodie bags, filled with products from the companies who advertise on her website. She passes them out, then slides into a wet suit and paddles out to Black Rock to join the other volunteers.

The rest of the day goes by in a blur. When the buses finally arrive, fifty exhausted, sandy kids stagger on, laughing and waving. Rae waves back. She knows she's given them a day they will never forget.

As she walks back to the beach to begin cleaning up, she notices her mother and Bonnie Gormley sitting together at a picnic table, talking intently. Rae crosses her fingers. "Put in a few good words for me," she whispers.

"Rae, we've got a problem," Luna says, walking up with Kanani, Isobel, and Cricket. Beside them is a hottie in a Sola Beach Lifeguard T-shirt, and he's holding Barrels, who is wagging his tail and licking his face.

"Hi, my name is Drew," he says. "I didn't want to bother you while the kids were here, but this is my dog."

"*Your* dog?" Rae gasps.

"Like I told your friends, I rescued him from a shelter less than a year ago. Then Barney and I got separated at Gubanador Mesa recently."

"Barney?" Rae repeats weakly. "His name is Barney?"

"Yes. I looked and looked—even came back the next day—but I couldn't find him. I thought he was lost forever, until now."

Rae swallows hard. Gubanador Mesa is about a mile north of Carson Beach. "Didn't you see our flyers?" she asks. "We put up a lot of lost dog flyers."

"I'm afraid not," Drew says. "I live in Sola Beach. I don't get up to Crescent Cove very often."

"He even has a photo of himself with Barrels—I mean, Barney," Isobel says sadly.

"Oh." Rae sighs. "Well, I guess he's yours, then."

"I saw how well trained he is now," Drew says, smiling at Rae. "I can't believe it. Barney was completely out of control when I got him. I owe you big time for that—and for taking such good care of him."

"We love him," Rae says with conviction.

"He obviously loves you, too," Drew replies. "That's why I almost wasn't going to say anything. But I really miss him." His voice trails off, and he shrugs.

"It's okay," Rae says, and she means it. "You're supposed to have him."

Drew looks relieved. "You can come visit him any time you want. Maybe a little surfing safari? We've got some good breaks down in Sola Beach."

The girls agree to give Drew and Barney some time to reconnect. Then, in a month or so, they'll plan a trip to visit him. "And to surf," Rae adds.

"Great," Drew says. "I'll take you to my secret spot."

Their eyes meet, and Rae notices that Drew's are deep and brown. She can't figure out why, but her heart is starting to pick up speed. Probably just the thought of saying good-bye to Barney, she decides.

She turns away and takes a deep breath. The beach is littered with sand toys, Frisbees, footballs, juice boxes, helmets, surf booties, and more. "What are we standing here for?" she asks, suddenly aware that she sounds just like her mother—but not really minding at all. "We've got work to do!"

18

*D*awn. The sky is a gray bowl sprinkled with stars, but at the horizon, the feathery clouds are turning pink. Rae pulls her car into the parking lot at Crescent Cove Beach Park and gets out. Glassy four-foot waves are rolling across the bay. She smiles and takes a deep breath. She's waited a long time for this moment.

Finally, when she can stand the anticipation no longer, she takes her board off her car and waxes it. She slips into her wet suit, straps on her leash, and now she's walking, faster . . . faster . . .

By the time Rae reaches the water, she's running, whooping as she jumps on her board and paddles through the shorebreak. Just last night Mom agreed to let her start surfing again. All she had to do was promise she wouldn't drop out of high school to join the tour. Okay, she can agree to that. After all, Bonnie Gormley waited until she graduated from college, and she was a world champion.

Rae paddles out to Black Rock and sits on her board, enjoying the feel of being in the water again. She loves everything about it—the taste of salt water on her lips, the sound of the water softly lapping against her board, the sight of a cormorant stretching his neck as he swallows a fish.

Here comes a wave! Rae takes it, and as she drops down the face and bottom-turns, she feels a rush of joy so intense it makes her laugh. Grinning, she flies up the wave, cuts back hard, then straightens out and makes the section. She's sailing now, just letting the wave take her as far as it will go.

"Yeah, girl! You go!"

It's Luna, paddling out. Kanani, Isobel, and Cricket are close behind. Rae lifts her arms in triumph. She's back where she belongs, and it feels good!

"Dad? It's Rae."

The session has ended and surf camp is about to begin. While the other girls sit in the sand, talking and relaxing, Rae is in her car, calling her father on her cell phone.

"Hi, hon. Are you okay? Where are you?"

"I'm fine, Dad. I'm sorry to bother you at work. It's just that I have something important to tell you."

"Yes?"

"I'm not moving to Chicago. I just can't. It's not that I don't want to be with you. I miss you something fierce. It's just . . . I belong here in California. I can't live without the surf."

She can hear her father sigh. "I understand. Sherri feels the same way, except it's the horses she can't live without."

"But we both want to visit you. Mom suggested Labor Day weekend. Do you think we could come out then?"

"I don't see why not." His voice sounds lighter now, more cheerful. "We'll take a city tour, visit some museums, go to a ball game. Maybe I could even arrange a father-daughter windsurfing lesson on Lake Michigan."

Rae doesn't have to fake her excitement. "That would be awesome!" she declares.

"I love you, Ray of Sunshine."

"I love you, too, Dad. Bye."

Rae hangs up and just sits there, contemplating the rest of her summer. Surfing in Crescent Cove. Windsurfing in Chicago. Maybe even a trip to Florida to go longboarding with Luna and her parents. She smiles. Things are turning out just fine.

"Flying through a hollow tube, sailing on a wave of wind. There's always surf in my life," Rae sings.

She plays a few more experimental chords and tries another line. "Closeouts that come crashing down, don't give up, just paddle out. There's always surf in my life."

Yeah, this new song is working out. She plays it again, then adds a chorus.

Life is a wave and I wanna keep surfin' it.
Day after day, I know this is my turf and it's
Okay, it's all right, it's fine.

She closes her eyes and imagines herself singing the song at the Open Mike Night at Java Jones. She's been daydreaming about that a lot lately, and thinking maybe Shane was wrong when he said she wasn't ready. Luna thinks she's good enough. Anyway, how will she ever know if she doesn't try?

The phone rings and she puts down her guitar to answer it. "Hello?"

"Rae Perrault?" A male voice, vaguely familiar.

"Uh-huh. Who's this?"

"Drew Hammel. I'm Barney's owner. We met at the beach thing."

Instinctively, Rae sits up a little straighter and brushes her hair out of her eyes. "Oh, hi."

"You're going to think this is crazy, but I had to call you."

"Why? Is something wrong with Barrels—I mean, Barney?"

"No, he's fine. It's just, well, that day on the beach when we met . . . I can't forget it."

"For sure," she agrees. "It was an amazing day. I don't know who was more stoked—the kids or the volunteers."

"No, I mean I can't forget *you*."

"Me?" She gulps.

"There's something about you," he says. "I don't know what it is. Maybe the fact that you thought up that whole event and made it happen. Or maybe it's the light shining from your eyes. All I know is I took one look at you and I said, 'I need to know this girl.' "

Rae's heart is beating so fast she can barely speak. "Wow," she whispers.

"Yeah, wow. So what do you think, Rae? Would you like to meet and take Barney for a walk? Maybe do a little surfing afterward?"

She pictures Drew's soft brown hair and dark chocolate eyes. She remembers the way he grinned when Barney licked his face. "I'd like that," she says.

They make a plan to meet that Saturday at Paintball

Point. After they hang up, Rae picks up her guitar again. Her voice rings out clear and true as she sings the chorus of her new song.

Life is a wave and I wanna keep surfin' it.
Day after day, I know this is my turf and it's
Okay, it's all right, it's fine.

And the future, she adds to herself. *That part is going to be great!*